This book should b
Lancashire County L

− 8 AUG
1 3 AUG

D1099748

MOLLIE
CINNAMON
IS NOT A
CUPCAKE

Lancashire County Library

30118130490794

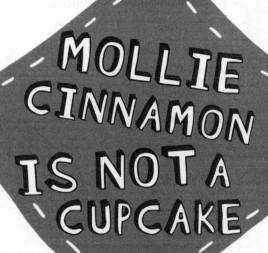

MOLLIE CINNAMON IS NOT A CUPCAKE

Sarah Webb

**WALKER
BOOKS**

Lancashire Library Services	
30118130490794	
PETERS	JF
£5.99	12-Jun-2015
NST	

This is a work of fiction. Names, characters, places and incidents
are either the product of the author's imagination or, if real, used
fictitiously. All statements, activities, stunts, descriptions, information
and material of any other kind contained herein are included for
entertainment purposes only and should not be relied on
for accuracy or replicated as they may result in injury.

First published 2015 by Walker Books Ltd
87 Vauxhall Walk, London SE11 5HJ

2 4 6 8 10 9 7 5 3 1

Text © 2015 Sarah Webb
Cover photographs © 2015 Maja Topcagic
and Judy Davidson / Getty Images
Little Bird Island map by Jack Noel

The right of Sarah Webb to be identified as author of this work
has been asserted by her in accordance with the Copyright,
Designs and Patents Act 1988

This book has been typeset in Berkeley

Printed and bound in Great Britain by Clays Ltd, St Ives plc

All rights reserved. No part of this book may be reproduced,
transmitted or stored in an information retrieval system in any
form or by any means, graphic, electronic or mechanical,
including photocopying, taping and recording, without prior
written permission from the publisher.

British Library Cataloguing in Publication Data:
a catalogue record for this book is available from the British Library

ISBN 978-1-4063-4835-4

www.walker.co.uk

Dear Reader,

I've always loved books about islands: Enid Blyton's *Five on a Treasure Island* and *The Secret Island*; the wonderful Irish adventure *Island of the Great Yellow Ox* by Walter Macken; the Anne of Green Gables books, which are set on Prince Edward Island in Canada; and a very old book called *The Swiss Family Robinson*, which my mum used to read to me, and is about a family who are stranded on a desert island.

A few years ago, I stayed in a yurt (a round Mongolian tent) on a small island called Cape Clear. It was so quiet, so peaceful. There was no traffic noise, only the odd dog barking and birds calling. One night as I lay on the grass, looking at the stars – there were so many glittering above me that I saw not one but *two* shooting stars – I started to think about what it might be like to live on a small island.

I decided I'd like to create and write stories about my very own island, Little Bird. At its heart would be a very special cafe, the Songbird Cafe – a place where everyone on the island meets. And then I introduced Mollie Cinnamon, a girl who is used to city life, and I stood back and watched the island's magic cast its spell on her.

I hope you have the chance to visit a stunning island like Cape Clear one day. Until then, you can read about Mollie and her journey from city slicker to island girl.

Best and many wishes,
Sarah XXX

P. S. For teacher's notes on using *Mollie Cinnamon Is Not a Cupcake* in the classroom, see www.SarahWebb.ie.

MAINLAND

SEAFIRE
POINT

HORSESHOE
BAY

SUNNY

LOUGH
CARA

BLIND
HARBOUR

CARA
WOODS

SOUTH
HARBOUR

FASTNET
LIGHTHOUSE

RED ROCK
VILLAGE

The
Songbird
Cafe

RED MOLL'S
CASTLE

BULL
ISLAND

LITTLE
BULL

MOLLIE

THE ATLANTIC

N
W   E
S

Little
Bird
Island

Chapter 1

As I watch from the window of the ferry, Little Bird Island gets bigger and bigger. I can just make out the harbour, and behind it, a stone castle covered in ivy, where Red Moll McCarthy once lived. She was a famous pirate queen and Granny Ellen said she is one of our ancestors. I was named after them both – Mollie Ellen Cinnamon.

There's a village just up from the harbour, the buildings all painted bright seasidey colours: strawberry pink, vanilla yellow, mint green. I can't believe I'm about to be imprisoned on a tiny island in the middle of nowhere with people who think it's normal to paint their house the colour of ice cream! And Little Bird is such a weird name for an island. It sounds like something from *Sesame Street*. I'm doomed.

Flora dropped me at the bus terminal this morning and made the driver promise to keep an eye on me. Then she had the nerve to get all bleary-eyed and emotional.

"I'm going to miss you, Mollie Mops," she said, hugging me so tight I could barely breathe. "I'll say hello to the kangaroos and wallabies for you. Be good for your great-granny, OK? And email me all your news, promise? Sorry I can't travel with you, but I have so much packing to do. You know what I'm like, darling, last minute dot com."

"Don't forget your passport this time," I said. "It's in the fruit bowl on the kitchen counter, remember?"

She gave one of her tinkling laughs and squeezed me even closer. "How am I going to survive without you? I miss you already, sweetie. See you in three weeks for our Parisian adventure." And then she kissed the tip of my freckled nose, and off she skipped, abandoning me, her only daughter, to my fate.

At first the bus ride wasn't too bad – most of it was on the motorway – but the journey along the coast took for ever, worse luck. The roads were so winding and bumpy that I felt really sick. When we finally got to the ferry terminal, the bus driver insisted on walking me to the boat, like I was five. It was so embarrassing.

The journey across the sea took about forty lumpy minutes and now the mainland is a grey-and-green curve behind us. The little ferry has just docked. Flora told me to stay on it and that my great-granny would come and find me. So I wait alone in the cabin, surrounded by cardboard boxes and oddly shaped packages.

The ferry is ancient and smells of diesel fumes and rotten fish. I'm dying to get off, so I jump up from the orange plastic seat and stick my head through the doorway, almost crashing into a white-haired woman.

"Oops, careful, child," she says. "Mollie? Is that you?" She has a strong accent, all sing-songy.

I nod.

She smiles, making her bright blue eyes twinkle. "I'm your great-granny. Call me Nan. Everyone does. You're very welcome to Little Bird. It's wonderful to finally meet you in person."

I'm not sure what I was expecting from my great-granny, but it wasn't a petite woman in muddy green wellies with a long white plait down her back. Flora's tall and so was Granny Ellen.

"Have you got your bags, child?" she asks me.

She's called me child twice now. How old does she think I am? I may be small for my age, but I'm nearly thirteen. I don't say anything, just nod. I know it's a bit rude, but it feels really weird being here.

I've spoken to Nan on the phone a few times recently (which was super Awkward with a capital *A*), but I've never met her in person. She and Flora don't exactly get on, which is another reason why being here is strange. I guess Flora was so desperate to get rid of me she'd have sent me anywhere.

I swing my rucksack over my shoulder and pick up my travel bag. "What *is* all this?" I ask as I almost trip over a rectangular package that must be at least three metres long.

"That's a tree," Nan says. "The smaller boxes are probably books or DVDs. Everything that comes to the island is dropped off by ferry. There's no postal service, so Alanna takes in the packages, rings the people they belong to and they come and collect them."

"Who's Alanna?"

Instead of answering my question, Nan asks, "Are you hungry?"

"A bit." I'm starving. We left the apartment at nine and it's now four. There wasn't any bread in the house so I couldn't make sandwiches. All I've had today are an apple and a packet of crisps. Flora says I'm a demon if I haven't been fed. She's the opposite – she often forgets to eat. She can go a whole day on one piece of toast.

"In that case you're about to meet Alanna in person," Nan says. She leaps off the ferry deck and then scrambles up the old stone steps in the harbour wall like a mountain goat. She walks towards a tiny cream Fiat 500 that is parked a few metres away. I follow her, my stuffed bag hitting my shins with every step.

She points over at a sky-blue building. "That's Alanna's place – the Songbird Cafe."

The cafe looks nice. It has a wooden sign swinging over the door and white tables outside with matching chairs. There's a wooden conservatory to the left, a big window overlooking the harbour at the front and a cluster of metal dog bowls near the door.

Besides the cafe, there is a tourist office, a craft shop, a pub called The Islander's Rest and a small grocery shop. And that's it. There must be another village on the island, a bigger one.

"Are you all right, Mollie?" Nan asks me. "You're being very quiet."

No, I'm not all right – I miss Dublin and Flora already. But I don't know Nan at all and I don't want to talk to her about this stuff. I gulp down the lump in my throat, nod again and say, "Fine."

"Let's get your bag in the car then," she says, her voice all bright and chirpy.

After putting my bag in the boot of her little car, we head to the cafe. I clutch my rucksack against my chest, needing to keep something from home close by me. It's quiet on the island, so different to the city, and I'm starting to feel very alone and lost – like the little alien E.T., abandoned on planet earth. I don't know anyone here. What was Flora thinking? I can't believe she's leaving me here for two whole months.

"What do you like doing in Dublin?" Nan asks me as we walk to the cafe. "Are you into sport?"

"Not really."

"What are you interested in then? Music? Writing? Drama?"

"Nothing, really." Which is a complete lie. Movies are my life. I just don't feel like answering her right now.

"Come on, you must like something. How about television? Do you watch your mum when she's on?"

"Sometimes," I admit. My mum, Flora Cinnamon, is a television presenter. She started off doing the "continuity", which means talking between the shows – you know, "Gosh, wasn't that exciting? Stay tuned for more drama in *EastEnders*, coming up next." Then she was a weather girl for a few years, and she's just landed a job presenting a new holiday programme called *Travelling Light*. She'll be filming in amazing cities all over the world: Paris, Rome, New York. The first stop is Sydney, Australia, and then Auckland, New Zealand. Unfortunately she can't take me with her as I'd miss too much school. That's why I'm on Little Bird being interrogated by Nan.

I'm dreading attending the local school while I'm staying here. I won't know a soul. But here's the good news – Flora's promised to take me to Paris with her in three weeks' time. We have it all worked out. She's going to come and collect me. We'll spend the weekend together in Paris and I'll get to watch her filming some of her show in the most romantic city in the world – imagine! I can't wait. Flora's always really busy with work and her friends and we don't get to spend much time together just the two of us, so it's going to be ultra special. She's promised we can visit the lock bridges – where lovers put their initials on a padlock and secure it to the metal railings of the bridge, pledging their *amour* for ever (how swoony is that?). And we're going to see the Eiffel Tower.

"She's doing very well, isn't she, your mum?" Nan says, interrupting my thoughts. "I love watching her. When's her new show on the telly?"

"It starts in May, I think. Flora isn't quite sure."

"Flora? Is that what you call her?"

"Yes. She says 'Mum' makes her feel old." Flora's twenty-nine. She had me when she was seventeen and she's always telling me how young she is to be a mum.

Nan smiles. "If 'Mum' sounds old, then 'Great-Granny' sounds positively ancient. I can't believe I have a great-granddaughter who's so grown up." She pauses for a second, then says, "Mollie, I know this must be difficult for you, but I'm delighted to have you here. I've wanted to meet you for a very long time now. I think you'll like Little Bird."

"I doubt it. Flora says it's the most boring place in the universe." The words are out of my mouth before I can stop them and I instantly feel bad.

Nan just gives a surprised laugh and says, "Your mum is a bright-lights, big-city kind of girl. Like my Ellen was. But I know Ellen loved the island in her own way, and maybe you'll grow to love it too."

Granny Ellen was Flora's mum. Which makes her Nan's daughter. She died two years ago. I wish Nan wouldn't talk about Granny Ellen. I don't like thinking about her – it makes me too sad. But I don't say anything. Nan wouldn't understand. Flora says they weren't close.

"It's quiet here, but you'll get used to it," Nan adds. "And the harbour and the village can get quite busy in the summer."

"There are other shops, right?" I ask. "Places to buy clothes and stuff? A cinema? A Chinese?" I love Chinese noodles.

"Mollie, it's a small island. The population's tiny – less than two hundred. Everyone orders what they need from the Internet. We're very lucky – the island has a broadband connection every Saturday. We all trek down to the library and queue up to use the one computer on Little Bird."

"What?"

She smiles. "Ha! Got you. We have broadband in the house. Don't look so horrified. We're not all that backward. If you need clothes, we can order them online, and I have lots of movies on DVD." She pushes open the door to the cafe. "Now let's get you some food. Ellen used to get really ratty if she hadn't eaten. Are you the same?"

"No!" I say, a little too loudly.

Nan laughs. "Of course not."

Chapter 2

The old-fashioned bell over the door tinkles as we walk into the cafe. I'm hit by the smell of baking, which reminds me of Granny Ellen again. My eyes start to sting with tears. Luckily Nan doesn't seem to notice.

Granny Ellen never talked about Nan. Flora says they had some sort of mega argument a long time ago. I wasn't allowed to ask Granny Ellen about it. That's why I've never been to Little Bird before or met Nan. The last time Flora was on the island was for her grandpa's funeral when she was fifteen, and she hasn't been back since.

Granny Ellen used to look after me while Flora was working and I loved hanging out with her. She'd help me with my homework and we'd bake together – she loved making cakes. She died two years ago of a brain haemorrhage. One of the neighbours found her collapsed at her front door, but it was too late by then. I was so upset I went quiet for days and I couldn't eat a thing. Flora was really worried about me because I was just so sad. How could someone be there one minute, perfectly healthy, and then gone the next? It didn't make sense. I still miss her every day.

Some nights I dream about Granny Ellen. We're doing ordinary things like watching old movies or baking together. Then I wake up and realize that she's gone and I cry.

Suddenly a warm hand touches mine as a dark-haired girl presses a white paper napkin into my palm. I quickly dab my eyes and then shove the napkin into my pocket before Nan sees.

"Hiya, Nan," the girl says, giving Nan a warm hug. She's amazing looking – willowy, with an oval face and strong, cat-like cheekbones. She could be a supermodel if she wasn't so small. She has the most incredible emerald-green eyes, with tiny flecks of gold dancing around the pupils. For a second I'm lost in them.

"Alanna, this is Mollie," Nan says.

"You're very welcome to the Songbird, Mollie," Alanna says. "It's great to have you on the island. Come in and say hi whenever you feel like it." From the kind look in the girl's eyes, I know Nan's been telling her all about me. How I'm only staying here because my mum can't find anyone else to mind me for so long. How I don't have a dad to stay with.

Her pity makes me bristly and irritated. I don't need anyone feeling sorry for me. I adjust my rucksack, which is heavy on my shoulder, and look at the squashy leather sofa by the window. "Can I have a hot chocolate with marshmallows and a croissant, please? Do I have to come up and collect it?"

Alanna looks taken aback. "No, I'll bring it over to you."

"Thanks." As soon as I sit down I realize how rude I've been. Alanna was only trying to be friendly and welcoming. I'm such an idiot.

Nan continues talking to Alanna, and I catch snippets of their conversation. They don't know I have super hearing.

"Sorry about that," Nan is saying. "She's tired and I think she's a wee bit homesick."

"That's OK. I understand."

"Any news from the bank, pet?"

Alanna sighs. "They're going over your figures, but it doesn't look good."

"Can they not see how important this place is to Little Bird? The cafe can't close – it's the island's heart. And it's your home. They have no right to—" Nan stops suddenly.

"Are you OK, Nan?" Alanna asks.

"Just a touch of angina," she says, wincing. "I've been getting it a lot lately. Nothing to worry about." She notices me watching and I look away quickly.

I can't make out anything else as they've lowered their voices, but, as Granny Ellen used to say, I can feel my ears burning. They're obviously talking about me again. Great – just what I need. And from the sound of things, this cafe is closing down, which is a shame because it's quite cosy and pretty. Not that it really matters to me. In two months I'm out of here!

Nan walks towards me. "I'm just popping outside to ring Flora. Let her know you've arrived. Would you like to speak to her?"

My eyes start to well up at the mention of Flora's name and I blink the tears away. "Maybe later."

"I understand. I won't be long, pet."

So here I am, alone again. My phone is out of battery, so I can't text my best friend, Shannon, and I've left my book – *Hollywood Movie Stars of the 1950s* – in my other bag. It's one of Granny Ellen's old books. Flora says it's too grown up for me, but it's really interesting and full of cool black-and-white photos of people like Audrey Hepburn and Grace Kelly. Granny Ellen was mad about 1950s movie stars. She always said they don't make actresses like they used to. She loved their glossy hair and glamorous clothes. "Real women with real curves," she'd say. "Not like those modern movie stars who look like they'd fall down a drain. No, give me Marilyn Monroe or Maureen O'Hara any day."

To stop myself getting sad about Granny Ellen again, I look around the cafe. Chains of funny-looking straw dolls, joined together by their little straw hands, are strung across the walls and the window, and there's a doll on every table, resting against the salt and pepper holders. All the dolls are dressed in white cotton skirts and green cloaks. Weird.

The place is empty apart from a man and a woman on the far side of the room speaking another language – Italian, I think. It's not like the cafe down the road from our apartment, which is always buzzing.

"So you're a movie buff?" Alanna slides a hot chocolate and a croissant onto the coffee table in front of me. "Mind if I sit down for a second?"

I shake my head, unnerved by her first question. How on earth did she know…?

As if reading my mind, Alanna nods at the button badges pinned to my rucksack. "Audrey Hepburn, Judy Garland and the ruby slippers from *The Wizard of Oz*. Old school – a girl after my own heart. It's from the 1930s, that film. I'm surprised you know it."

"I used to watch it with my granny. It's my favourite film."

"I love it too. So what brings you to the island, Mollie?"

I hesitate. I'm sure Nan has already told her and she's just being polite.

"Sorry, you probably want to eat your croissant in peace." She starts to get up.

"No, it's OK," I say quickly. "Flora, that's my mum, is away working, so I'm staying with Nan. Flora's a television presenter. She's working on a new travel show for RTÉ and she's leaving for Sydney tomorrow and then Auckland."

"Lucky her," Alanna says. Often when I tell people about Flora's job they're very impressed, but Alanna doesn't seem all that awed by it. "New Zealand is magic. I did the whole camper-van thing a few years ago. Whale watching, glaciers, smelly mud springs – the works. It was an amazing trip."

I'm surprised. She doesn't look all that grown up, but maybe that's because she's so small. She must be at least eighteen if she's running her own cafe. "On your own?" I ask her. "Or with your parents?"

Before Alanna can answer, the Italian woman appears beside us. "May I order another Americano, please? Your coffee is very good."

Alanna jumps to her feet. "Of course."

"We have heard about your dolphin," the woman continues. "Do you think he will be here today?"

Dolphin? Flora never said anything about a dolphin. I sit up a little.

"I think he just might," Alanna says. "Let me pop outside and have a look for you." She smiles at me. "Nice talking to you, Mollie."

"You too." I try to smile back at her, but I don't think it reaches my eyes. I'm still feeling pretty homesick.

After eating my croissant, which is delicious, I cup my hands around the hot chocolate and look out of the window. A few small fishing boats are bobbing up and down in the harbour, and tubby yellow-beaked seagulls are either perched on stone bollards or swooping over the water. OK, it's all very pretty and quaint and everything, but it's so quiet. What do people around here do for fun?

I spot Alanna on the pier. Her hands are held up to her mouth and she seems to be calling to someone on one of the fishing boats. And then I see something in the water at the mouth of the harbour – a pale grey curve. I lean forwards and squint. It's a dolphin!

It leaps out of the water and I almost squeal with excitement. I've never seen a dolphin before. Not in real life. There's a pod of dolphins living in Killiney Bay and Flora's always promising to take me to see them, but she never has. Animals aren't really her thing. I smile a real smile, and for a moment I feel happy.

"That's Click," Nan says, coming up to me. "He lives in the bay. Beautiful, isn't he?"

"Yes."

He disappears under the waves. I watch for a moment, but he doesn't come back up again.

"Your mum sent you lots of hugs and kisses. She wishes you were flying out with her."

"Did Flora really say that?" Flora made it quite clear that I couldn't go to Australia and New Zealand, full stop. And believe me, I spent days trying to change her mind.

Nan blushes. "She didn't use those exact words, but I'm sure that's what she meant. She's a bit frantic with all the packing."

I stay quiet. I know exactly what Flora is like when she's obsessed with a new job or going away. And this time it's both. The third thing that makes her all flustered and forgetful is a brand-new boyfriend. At least she doesn't have one of those.

"Don't be too hard on your mum, child," Nan says. "She's nervous about this new job and it's making her a bit … caught up with herself. It doesn't mean that she isn't thinking about you. Ellen was just the same. It was all rush, rush, rush when she was excited about something."

Eager to change the subject, I ask her, "What's with all the dolls?"

"It's St Brigid's Day. Don't you celebrate it at home?"

I wrinkle up my nose. "No! Who's St Brigid?"

Nan tuts. "Do they teach you nothing in school these days? St Brigid is an Irish saint. There is also a Celtic goddess of fertility and nature called Brigid. We celebrate both the saint and the coming of spring today, the first of February. The little dolls are called Brideógs and you can make a wish on one. Try it." Nan passes me a little doll. "Hold her tight and make a wish."

I stare at the strange doll in my hands. Granny Ellen was very superstitious. She always saluted single magpies to ward off bad luck. She avoided walking under ladders and stepping on cracks in the pavement and picked up pins and "lucky pennies" all the time. She also made wishes on all kinds of things: shooting stars, rainbows, engagement rings. Granny Ellen would definitely make a wish.

I want to tell Nan that wishing is stupid. I've made dozens of wishes before – quite serious ones – and they've never come true. But thinking of Granny Ellen has softened me a little. Maybe just this once my wish will come true.

I close my eyes. *Take me home.*

Chapter 3

Nan's house is called Summer Cottage. It doesn't take long to get there. We drive up a small road and then turn right onto a muddy track with grass growing down the middle and bushes and trees on either side. Set back from the lane is a white two-storey house. I'm not sure what I was expecting – a falling-down farmhouse with hens pecking around the yard and mud everywhere, maybe – but it wasn't this.

"Here we are," Nan says. "What do you think?"

I take in the pale blue door and window frames, the flower pots full of nodding white snowdrops, the weeping willow tree in the middle of the large garden and the small wooden pagoda at the far end, which looks perfect for hiding away in and reading. There's even a gurgling stream running down the side of the garden, with a small humpback bridge over it. The whole place is like something out of a fairy tale.

I shrug. "It looks OK."

Nan's mouth twitches. "Glad you approve."

Inside, the house is modern and bright and smells just like Granny Ellen's house – a mixture of baking and fresh flowers.

It's warm too. Flora is always forgetting to pay the gas bill, so sometimes we don't have heating for days and the apartment is so cold you can blow out puffs that hang in the air like dragon's breath. Plus, the communal hallway smells of curry and bins. At least our apartment smells nice as Flora always has a scented candle on the go. She once blew a month's grocery money on a posh Jo Malone one that smelled of orange blossom. Granny Ellen said Flora has champagne taste on a lemonade budget.

Nan closes the front door behind me. "Leave your bag at the end of the stairs," she tells me. "I'll show you the kitchen first."

I follow her down the hall. The right-hand wall is full of framed photographs. They're mainly pictures of the island, and of a stocky red-haired man. In one photo he's wearing an old-fashioned black teacher's cloak over a tweedy suit, like one of the professors in Harry Potter. He's grinning, making his eyes go all crinkly.

"That's PJ," Nan says, following my gaze. "Your great-grandpa. He ran the island's primary school. Have you never seen a photo of him?"

I shake my head. "Did Flora meet him?" I never met my own grandad, Granny Ellen's husband. He was much older than she was and he died before I was born.

Nan goes quiet for a second. "It was complicated. Ellen wasn't keen on island life. She wanted something different. After she left Little Bird she only came back a handful of times when your mum was little. Flora did meet him, but she may not remember very clearly. She was at his funeral, all right, but Ellen and I—" Nan stops abruptly. "It's all in the past now, child. No need to burden you with it. Let's just say that Ellen and I quarrelled and I regret it deeply. I'm a stupid, stubborn old woman and your granny was a wonderful person." She smiles at me. Then she points at another photo. "You're the spit of her at that age. She was about eleven when I took that one."

Granny Ellen is sitting cross-legged on a beach towel, a comic resting on her knees. Her head is turned towards the camera, showing her dark blue eyes, nose dotted with freckles and wavy, flaming-red hair. Nan's right – it's like looking in a mirror.

"Where was the photo taken?" I ask. "Is that beach on the island?"

"That's Horseshoe Bay, down near the harbour. We swim there when the weather is better. Now, I can smell that stew. I hope it's not burning. This way."

I look at Nan's photos a moment longer before following her. They're good. Really good. Like images you'd see in a magazine. I think about telling her that, but I suddenly feel shy. I know I've been a bit stand-offish since I got here. I need to be nicer, to say thank you once in a while. Granny Ellen was big on manners.

The kitchen is cosy, with a cream Aga, sky-blue cupboards and a dresser full of hand-painted pottery. There's a wooden table in the centre of the room and an alcove in one corner with a desk and a laptop.

"I spend most of my time in here," Nan says, planting her bum against the Aga. "I love baking. Does Flora cook?"

"She's too busy. She's the takeaway queen of Dublin."

Nan laughs. "I see. And what about you? Do you like to cook?"

"Sometimes." Actually, I love cooking, but I don't get much chance any more. I used to do lots of baking at Granny Ellen's house, but the kitchen in our apartment is tiny – more like a cupboard than a room – and the electric cooker barely works. Plus, cooking wouldn't be the same without Granny Ellen.

Nan checks the stew, which smells delicious. My stomach gurgles.

"We'll eat very soon," Nan reassures me. "It just needs another twenty minutes or so. Would you like to see the rest of the house while we're waiting?"

"Sure. I mean, yes, please."

I follow Nan down the hallway again. There's a small study full of packed bookshelves and a living room with a black pot-bellied stove and a squashy cream sofa. There's also a huge flat screen TV. I smile when I spot it.

"Not so stuck in the dark ages, am I, child?" Nan says, nodding at the telly. "I love watching movies on a decent-sized screen – it makes it more like the cinema. Do you like films?"

"Yes," I say.

"Ellen loved films. It must run in the family. I thought we could have a proper cinema night once a week. With popcorn and hot dogs. You can pick the film. Nothing too noisy or action-packed, mind. I'm not a big fan of films with lots of explosions or screechy-tyre car chases. Classics are more my thing. Right, let's get you settled into your room. It's up the wooden hill."

That's something Granny Ellen used to say – "wooden hill" instead of "stairs". And "heavens to Betsy" for "oh dear." That one always made me laugh.

As soon as I walk into the bedroom I know there's something funny about it. It looks perfectly normal, although I'm not loving the Disney-Princess-style canopy over the bed, but the room feels different to the rest of the house – older and musty, like it hasn't been lived in for a long time. Nan's acting oddly too. She's standing in the doorway with this stiff, forced smile on her face.

"This was Ellen's room," she says. "But it's yours now. No one's stayed in here for quite some time, so I'm sorry if it's a bit stuffy. I did air it, but…"

I shiver. I believe in ghosts, you see. I've never actually seen one, but that doesn't mean they don't exist. Granny Ellen believed in them too. "Don't be scared of the spirits, Mollie," she always said. "They're just souls waiting to pass into heaven. They don't mean us any harm. Think of them as guardian angels."

For a second I imagine that Granny Ellen is in the room watching me, maybe even smiling, her eyes twinkling, and I don't feel scared any more. How could I be afraid of Granny Ellen?

"Are you all right, child?" Nan asks.

I give myself a shake. "Just thinking about Granny Ellen," I say honestly.

"I understand. Ellen was special, all right – always the brightest thing in a room. PJ used to say there are people in this world and there are *people*." Nan presses her lips together, her eyes wet. "You must miss her."

I nod silently. I don't trust myself to say anything without crying.

"There's another room if you prefer," she says, "but it's awfully small."

"No, this one is nice."

"Good. And I can change anything you don't like."

Apart from the canopy, which is a bit young for me, the bedroom is lovely and it's much bigger than my room at home. It has a window seat, bookshelves and even a desk. I've never had my own desk before. I usually have to do my homework on the kitchen table.

On the wall above the desk is a framed painting of a woman with a shock of wild red hair. She's wearing a red wool cape and there's an ancient-looking curved gun tucked into her belt. I know exactly who she is – Red Moll, the famous Irish pirate queen.

"That picture belonged to your granny," Nan says. "PJ painted it for her. It's pretty good, isn't it?"

"Granny Ellen told me the old legends," I say.

"They're not legends, child – it's history. Red Moll was a

real person and she lived right here on this island."

"I know," I say. "I saw her castle from the ferry. Granny Ellen showed me pictures of it once, so I recognized it immediately."

"Did she tell you how Red Moll saved Little Bird from the Algerians?"

"Fighting off the slave traders, you mean?" It was one of Granny Ellen's favourite stories. She was obsessed with Red Moll. She even dragged me to a Red Moll re-enactment once. We had to dress up in costumes from the sixteen hundreds. She made them herself. She was Red Moll in a chestnut-brown linen tunic and a billowing red wool cloak (called a "bratt", which made me giggle), with a curved gun (a fake!) that she found on eBay tucked into her leather belt. I was one of her daughters in a matching outfit, but without the gun. Red Moll had three daughters and two sons, but because she was so busy as a pirate queen, she gave them to her sister to look after.

At the re-enactment we got to sail on a galley ship along the quays in Dublin and then we freed some "slaves" from another gang of people who were dressed up as Algerian slave traders. It was all a bit weird, but Granny Ellen loved it.

When I finish telling Nan about the re-enactment, she repeats the story I've heard so many times. "Those Algerians never knew what hit them. They were trying to raid Little Bird for slaves. Red Moll had been tipped off by a fisherman and she rounded up her men – over two hundred of them – and came tearing out of Dolphin Bay on one of her galley ships.

She commanded her crew to howl like banshees and wave their swords in the air. She scared those slave traders right back to Africa. It was a different story for the poor folk at Baltimore down the coast," she adds.

"What happened to them?"

"They didn't have Red Moll to defend them. Slave traders sailed in and captured over a hundred people. They sold them all in the Algerian slave markets. Only three made it back to Ireland alive. It was called the Sack of Baltimore. Didn't you do it in history class?"

I shake my head. "We never do anything interesting. Just the Greeks and the Romans and stuff. When did it happen? The Sack thing."

"In sixteen thirty-one. Ten years after Red Moll's death. They wouldn't have dared if she was still around. Those slave traders were all terrified of her. The English Navy, too. She was forever raiding English merchant ships. She used to fight sea battles for whoever would pay her the most. She even fought for the French at one stage. She was an amazing woman. I can see why Ellen loved her. And Flora must have caught the bug too, naming you after her."

"Granny Ellen told me they had a big fight about it. She wanted Flora to call me Moll, but Flora said it was too old-fashioned. So they settled on Mollie."

Then I think of something else Granny Ellen once said. "Did Red Moll really lift up a horse?"

Nan smiles. "It was a foal with a broken leg. It had fallen

down one of the cliffs on the far side of the island and she climbed down and rescued it."

"And we're really related to her?"

"Yes, we most certainly are."

I look out of the window at the bay where Red Moll sailed all those years ago.

"Ellen loved to sit and look out at the sea," Nan says. "She liked to imagine she was Red Moll, commanding her fleet." She pauses before saying, "Mollie, I know it must be hard on you – new place, new people, everything reminding you of your granny and how much you miss her. I miss her too."

She looks at me. I get the feeling I'm supposed to say something, but I can't think of anything. Of course I miss Granny Ellen – I miss her so much it hurts – but I don't feel able to talk about it with someone I hardly know.

When Nan realizes I'm not going to say anything, she continues, "Anyway, I'm pleased to have you here. No, more than pleased. I'm over the moon. I want to get to know you properly. We're family after all."

"I'm only here two months," I remind her yet again.

"Yes, of course," she replies quickly. "But in the meantime, I hope you'll be very happy here."

As soon as Nan's gone, I look around the room again. The white walls are so plain. Apart from the Red Moll painting and a small mirror by the door, they're completely bare. I open up my rucksack and take out my big yellow notebook. Tucked inside is my prized collection – my signed movie-star photographs. They used to belong to Granny Ellen. She didn't actually meet any of the movie stars, but she used to write to all their film studios and fan clubs and ask for autographs. She started doing it when she was a little girl. After she died, Flora wanted to sell them on the Internet. I nearly killed her. We had a big row and eventually she let me keep them. But I always carry them with me, just in case. I wish I could trust her, but you never know what Flora's going to do.

I arrange some of the photos on the desk: Elizabeth Taylor, Grace Kelly, Maureen O'Hara and Audrey Hepburn, all posing in different ways. Elizabeth Taylor is wearing a full-length crimson evening gown and smiling at the camera. Her eyes are the most amazing colour – almost violet. The picture of Grace Kelly is an elegant black-and-white head shot. Her hair is so perfectly styled in a ballerina's bun that it looks like it's been sprayed on. They're all dead now, apart from Maureen O'Hara, who's an old lady. She's Irish and has red hair like me.

The Audrey Hepburn photo is my favourite. Granny Ellen was only my age when she wrote to her, and Audrey sent her a photo of herself hugging a kitten. She signed it: "To my young Irish fan Ellen McCarthy. Fond regards, Audrey." I put that one on the bedside table, propped up against the reading lamp.

Then I take out my movie-star book and put it beside Audrey's photograph. After that I start to unpack my clothes, but I get bored of that pretty quickly. Instead I sit on the window seat and watch a bird flying past in the twilight. It's so quiet in this house. I listen out for Nan, but I can't hear her. In our apartment there's always some sort of noise: Flora chatting on her mobile or singing along to a song on the radio, our neighbours' baby crying, dogs barking outside, traffic. Here there's nothing. It's spooky and unnerving. Another world. I feel like Dorothy landing in Oz. I wish I had a little dog to hug, like she did. After picking up Audrey's photograph again, I run my fingers over the image of her cat. It's all I have.

"Toto, I've a feeling we're not in Kansas any more," I whisper.

Chapter 4

When I wake up the next morning, Nan's digital clock says it's 6 a.m. Six! I groan inwardly. Why does my body think it's time to get up? It's practically the middle of the night.

I didn't sleep very well because I kept having nightmares and then sitting up in a panic, my heart racing. In one of them all my teeth fell out and I swallowed them *and* a load of blood – yuck! In another I was dangling over the edge of a cliff. The earth was crumbling beneath my fingers and I was whispering, "Don't let go! Don't let go! Don't let go!" And then the ground gave way and I started to fall, but before I landed I woke up.

I try to go back to sleep, but it's no use. I'm wide awake. I lie in bed for a while reading my movie-star book. It's heavy and my arms start to ache from holding it sideways, so I sit up to read it, but then my shoulders get cold. Eventually I'm so chilly I climb out of bed and put on my hoodie. I draw back the curtains a little and peer out of the window. All I can see is inky blackness.

Then I take down a photo album from the bookshelves and open it. "Ellen, 11" is written on the inside cover in neat handwriting. There are two photos tucked under the plastic on the first page – faded colour snaps of Granny Ellen and my Great-Grandpa PJ playing football in Nan's garden. I recognize the stream and the humpback bridge in the background. I sit down at the desk and start to flick through the album. Some pages are empty, but the others are full of snapshots of Granny Ellen and PJ: digging rivers and dams on the beach; standing with arms around each other, squinting at the sun; PJ holding a spade proudly and Granny Ellen buried in the sand beside him, grinning, her body a mermaid's made out of sand. She has huge sand boobs covered with shells, and dark green seaweed hair. I smile to myself. It's a bit rude and funny, just the kind of thing me and Granny Ellen used to get up to on the beach near her house. Feeling a wave of sadness and longing for her, I pick up the album and kiss the photograph.

There's a knock on the door and Nan's head appears around it. "I thought I heard you stir," she says.

Startled, I drop the album, which falls onto the desk with a clatter. The mermaid photograph falls out.

"Sorry," I say, quickly slotting it back into place.

"Not to worry – nothing broken. Interesting, aren't they?"

I nod. I hope Nan didn't see me kissing Granny Ellen's photo. She'll think I'm a right baby. I can feel my cheeks hotting up.

But if she noticed she doesn't mention it. "You're up early. I thought teenagers were supposed to be nocturnal creatures. Especially at the weekend."

I stare down at the photo album. I don't want to tell her about my bad dreams so I stay silent.

When I don't reply, she adds, "I have dozens more albums downstairs if you ever want to take a look. We're so lucky having digital cameras and mobiles these days. Getting film developed used to cost me a fortune. Do you like taking photos?"

"Sometimes."

"You can borrow my camera if you like. It's a good one. It takes great pictures."

"Can you use it for taking videos?"

"Yes. Are you interested in making movies?"

I shrug. "Kind of. I've made a few Lego stop-motion animations with my friend Shannon, but they're not very good." My stomach rumbles. Even though I was ravenous last night my stomach felt funny, all knotted and twisty, so I couldn't eat much dinner. "Can I have some breakfast?"

"Of course. How about buttermilk pancakes?"

Granny Ellen used to make those too. I nod. "Yes, please. I'll just get dressed first."

Once Nan's gone, I rummage in my bag for my black jeans and my favourite black-and-white stripy top. I love black-and-white stripes. Granny Ellen used to say, "Here's my little zebra girl again," whenever I wore them.

Nan reminds me quite a lot of Granny Ellen. She went to a lot of trouble last night to make the dinner table look nice. She'd set it with sparkling glasses and cutlery, baby-blue place mats and matching napkins. I think she has a bit of a thing for blue! There was a vase of yellow flowers that looked like tiny daffodils and a (blue!) ribbon tied in a bow around the back of my chair. Granny Ellen was just the same. She loved using place mats and real napkins. She said it made people feel special and welcome. Flora's idea of setting the table is to open a Chinese takeaway carton and hand me a plastic fork. We mostly eat off our laps in front of the telly.

Dinner was delicious – beef and Guinness stew with mashed potatoes and then chocolate pots for dessert. It was a shame I couldn't eat much. Afterwards I asked if I could go straight to bed. Nan seemed a little disappointed. I think she wanted to ask me more questions about Dublin and Flora.

"Of course you can, child," she said. "It's been a long day for you. Don't let the bed bugs bite."

As I walk into the kitchen for breakfast, I can smell butter sizzling in a frying pan. Nan is at the Aga and there's a glass bowl on the counter beside her, half full of pale yellow batter mix.

"Would you like to make them while I set the table?" she asks.

"OK."

"Have you made buttermilk pancakes before, Mollie? Some people call them drop scones."

"Yes, lots of times," I say.

Nan smiles. "I'll put the plates out then. We'll make a good team, you and me. Wait and see."

Over breakfast Nan asks me if there's anything I'd like to do today.

I stop myself from saying, "Go home, please." Instead I shrug. "Not really. Maybe talk to Flora later."

Nan smiles. "I think we can arrange that. She said she'll ring us from the airport once they get to Singapore. It will be some time this evening. They have a two-hour stopover there before flying on to Sydney. In the meantime, I thought we could go to the cafe for a hot chocolate after lunch. I've invited a few of the girls from the island who are your age to come and meet you. Alanna's laying on some cupcakes."

My stomach clenches at the thought of meeting lots of strangers, and I chew on my lip.

"Don't look so worried, child," Nan says. "There are only four of them. Lauren, Chloe and Bonny all go to Bethlehem Heights – that's the senior school on the mainland where you'll be going. And I hope Sunny will come along, too, although she might not. She's very shy. She's home-schooled."

Four girls around my age – that doesn't sound too bad. But I'm still nervous.

The morning crawls by. That's what you get for being up with the birds, I guess. After helping Nan wash up (I remembered to offer. Granny Ellen would be proud of me), I finish unpacking my clothes and then sit down on the window seat, wondering what to do until lunchtime. Yet again there's nothing to see outside apart from birds and – yes, how exciting – a green tractor. I watch it trundle across one of the fields and then disappear down a laneway. I try ringing Shannon, but her phone isn't on, so I text her instead. *Hey, Shannon. What are you up to? It's really quiet here and I'm soooo bored. Are you going to basketball this morning? Mollie*

There's a knock on the door and Nan appears again. "How's the unpacking going?"

"I've finished."

"Good for you." I notice she's carrying another photo album. "When she was little, Ellen loved playing with paper dolls. She used to spend hours cutting them out and dressing them in different outfits. I kept her favourite ones. I thought you might like to take a look."

She hands me the album and I flick through the pages. Each plastic pocket holds a different cut-out doll: Audrey Hepburn in her black *Breakfast at Tiffany's* cocktail dress, Marilyn Monroe in a pink satin evening dress. I remember playing with paper dolls with Granny Ellen when I was little. They were quite fiddly – some of the tabs were tiny and I used to accidentally cut them off – but we loved doing them together. She also found dolly-dressing sticker books in a local bookshop, but I didn't like them as much. There's something very satisfying about cutting out the dresses yourself.

"I see you've got some of her movie-star photographs on your desk," Nan adds. "I'm glad they found a good home. They're very special, those photos. And I thought you might like to keep that too." She nods at the album.

"Thanks," I say, thinking of Flora. I'm so glad I stopped her selling them. And now I have something else to remind me of Granny Ellen. Maybe this morning won't be so bad after all.

"Mollie, this is Lauren," Nan says. I look at the girl sitting in the middle of the sofa at the Songbird Cafe. She's very pretty with a button nose and glossy chestnut-brown hair. She's flanked by two other girls, one dark-haired, the other blonde.

"And this is Chloe and Bonny," Nan adds. All three of them are wearing practically the same outfit: tracksuit bottoms low on their hips, tight sports tops with the collars turned up, unzipped hoodies and expensive trainers, like some sort of "sporty-cool" uniform. I feel self-conscious standing there in my jeans and stripy top.

The blonde girl, Bonny, gives me a friendly smile and says, "Hi, Mollie."

The other two are staring at me suspiciously as if I'm some sort of dangerous animal that should be in the zoo – a poisonous tree frog or a tarantula.

"Hi," Lauren says after a few seconds.

"Yeah, hi," Chloe adds.

"Why don't you join the girls, Mollie?" Nan gestures to the armchair opposite them and I sit down reluctantly.

"What are you all having?" she asks. "My treat."

"Cool, three skinny cappuccinos," Lauren says immediately. There's a long pause before she adds, "Please."

"And you, Mollie?" Nan says.

"Hot chocolate, please. With marshmallows and cream."

"Oh, can I have one of those instead?" Bonny says. "Sounds delicious. With extra marshmallows, please."

Lauren and Chloe roll their eyes at each other.

"Of course," Nan says. "Is Sunny here yet?"

"She's at her usual table," Bonny says, tilting her head towards the far side of the cafe, her curls bouncing like tiny springs.

I look in the direction Bonny indicated. There's a girl with long dark plaits sitting in the conservatory, watching us. As soon as I catch her eye she dips her head and starts scribbling in her notebook.

"Did you ask her to join you?" Nan asks.

Bonny opens her mouth to say something, but Lauren jumps in before she can speak.

"Of course we did," she says. "But I think she's cool over there."

"OK, as long as you asked," Nan says. "You can go over and say hello to Sunny later, Mollie. I'll just pop into the kitchen and give Alanna the order. Back in a minute."

As soon as Nan has gone, Chloe gives a snort. "So much for the diet, Bonny," she says. "Extra marshmallows? Really?"

Bonny goes red and starts playing with one of her curls. I feel sorry for her. She's bigger than the other girls, but she's certainly not fat.

"She's just trying to save you from yourself, babes," Lauren says. "You know that."

Bonny nods, but doesn't say anything. Then Lauren turns her attention to me. "Hey, Mollie, if Nan is your great-granny, how come you've never been to the island before?"

I shrug. "Flora, that's my mum, she loves the sun. We always go to hot places for our holidays, like Italy or the Caribbean." Flora is great at picking up these amazing last-minute holiday deals on the Internet. We never know where we're going till the day before we leave.

Bonny's eyes widen. "You've been to the Caribbean?"

"Yes, twice," I say. "We're going to Paris in three weeks too."

Bonny gasps. "I've always wanted to go to Paris. Lauren's mad about Paris, aren't you, Lauren?"

"No, I'm not," Lauren says.

"But you have that poster of the Eiffel Tower on the wall in your—" Bonny stops mid-sentence as Lauren glares at her.

"I used to like Paris," Lauren says. "But Paris is so over. The shops in Manhattan are way cooler."

"Have you been to New York?" I ask Lauren.

"No," she says. "But my mum says she'll take me next year."

"I thought you said you were going for your sixteenth," Chloe says.

Lauren gives her an icy look. "I've changed my mind."

"You're so lucky," Bonny says wistfully. "I've never been anywhere cool. Not even Dublin city."

I stare at her. "You've never been to Dublin? It's only a few hours away."

"I know!" Bonny says. "I keep telling my mum that, but she won't listen."

"I go into town every weekend with Flora," I say. "We practically live there. We go shopping and then catch a movie and eat in a restaurant." Every weekend is a bit of an exaggeration, but Lauren is starting to annoy me with her "Paris is so over" stuff.

"It sounds amazing," Bonny says.

"It *is* amazing," I say. "That's why I'm finding Little Bird so weird, I think. It's really quiet here, and what on earth do you do during the holidays? Birdwatching? Tractor spotting?"

Bonny's still smiling, but Lauren and Chloe's faces are stony.

"I mean, Little Bird's nice too," I add quickly. "All the lovely, um, nature and stuff." It sounds feeble even to my ears.

I'm insanely grateful when Nan reappears with Alanna just behind her carrying a tray.

"Two skinny cappuccinos and two hot chocolates, both with extra marshmallows," Alanna says, placing the Songbird Cafe mugs on the coffee table in front of us.

Nan is holding a cake stand with three tiers. She sets it carefully in the middle of the table.

"And a selection of my finest cupcakes," Alanna says, pointing at each delicious-looking layer. "Lemon drizzle, red velvet and the Songbird." The Songbird cakes look the best. Each one is covered in delicate pale blue icing with two tiny white wings rising out of the top. They're stunning.

Bonny is almost jumping up and down in her seat. Like

me, she's clearly a cupcake fan. "Thanks, Alanna," she says. "I'll go back on my diet tomorrow."

Alanna laughs. "Diet, schmiet. You don't need to diet, Bonny. You're perfect the way you are. Nothing wrong with a treat now and then. Enjoy, girls. I'm just going to borrow Nan's brain for a few minutes, but I'll see you in a little while."

I'm not sure I want to be alone with Lauren and Chloe any longer, especially after what I've just said about their precious island.

Nan squeezes my shoulder as if reading my mind. "I'm popping into the kitchen to help Alanna with her accounts. I won't be long, pet."

When she's gone, Lauren says, "I've just remembered, we all have to work on our school project. Isn't that right, girls?"

Bonny looks confused, but Chloe adds, "Yeah, an English project on our favourite writer. As if we actually have one." She gives a laugh.

"But that doesn't have to be finished until the end of term," Bonny says.

"My mum's making me work on it today," Lauren says. "*So* not cool."

"Mine too," Chloe says. "And yours said the same thing, Bonny, remember?"

Bonny still looks perplexed, but before she can say anything else Lauren starts wrapping the cupcakes up in napkins. "We'll take these to go. Come on, girls. Nice meeting you, Mollie."

"See you on the school ferry on Monday," Bonny says.

Lauren and Chloe are already practically out of the door. "Sorry we have to go," she adds.

"That's OK," I tell her. She seems nice. If I'd just kept my big mouth shut, maybe we could have been friends. I didn't mean to insult Little Bird – it just popped out. And now I've annoyed the only girls my age on the whole island. Great! I press my head into the back of the chair and close my eyes. When I open them again, Alanna is perched on the sofa arm.

"Nan says she'll be with you in a few minutes," she says. "She's looking over my accounts for me. She's really good with numbers. I see your new friends have skedaddled, along with my cupcakes. Everything all right?"

"Fine." I want to tell her what happened, but I don't want her to think badly of me. "They had homework to do."

"I see." From the knowing look in Alanna's eyes, I think she senses there's more to it than that, but she doesn't push it. "Why don't you join Sunny? I'll rustle up some more cupcakes."

I glance towards Sunny's table. Her head is still bowed over her book. "She seems busy," I say.

"Look again," Alanna says.

At that moment, the sun peeps out from behind the clouds, lighting up the conservatory and making it look even more bright and inviting. Sunny lifts her head and gives me a shy smile.

I follow Alanna into the conservatory.

"Sunny, this is Mollie," Alanna says. "Mollie, Sunny. Now,

Sunny doesn't talk, but she's an amazing artist and I'm sure she'll show you her work if you ask her."

Hang on. Did Alanna just say that Sunny doesn't talk? Is that supposed to be some sort of joke? I look around to ask Alanna what she means, but she's disappeared back into the kitchen.

Now that I think about it, Nan did warn me that Sunny is ultra shy. But that's OK – I understand shy. I can be quiet myself sometimes.

"Is it OK if I sit here?" I ask her.

She gives me another tiny smile and nods her head.

"Do you live here, on the island?"

She nods again.

"Have you always lived here?"

She shakes her head.

"Where did you live before?"

She blinks a few times, then stares down at her notebook again.

This is not going well. I try another yes or no question instead. At least she can reply to those. "Do you like it here?"

Another nod.

"Do you know Lauren and her friends?"

This time Sunny scrunches up her nose before nodding. She looks like she's just smelled something nasty, and it makes me laugh.

"At least Alanna seems nice."

A grin this time and a big nod.

"And the hot chocolate is good."

She nods another yes.

And then I'm stuck. I honestly can't think of another thing to ask her. We sit there for a minute – staring at each other, looking away, then staring again – until the silence becomes almost too much to bear. I bite my lip. It would be really rude to get up and leave, but this is so awkward.

Sunny must sense how I'm feeling. She turns the page of her book, which I see now is a sketchpad, and starts to draw. Her hand moves like a hummingbird's wing over the paper, making hundreds of hair-thin pencil lines. I watch, mesmerized. I've never seen anyone draw so quickly.

When she's finished, she pushes the book across the table towards me. Alanna was right. She's a really talented artist. She's drawn a comic strip – three different pictures in boxes. In the first one there are two little girls holding hands. Underneath are the words "Shenzhen, China". The smaller girl has a tiny ponytail sticking up from the top of her head, like a paintbrush. In the middle box is a plane, soaring over skyscrapers. And then, in the final box, an island shaped like a horseshoe with "Little Bird" written underneath.

I run my finger under each beautiful sketch. "You're from China originally," I say. "And you came to the island on a plane when you were little." I point to the girl with the cute ponytail.

Sunny shakes her head and points to the taller girl.

"That's you and your little sister then," I say. "And Little Bird is your home now."

She nods firmly.

"Were you adopted?" Oops, maybe that's a bit nosy.

But Sunny doesn't seem to mind. She just nods again.

"And you don't speak, ever?"

She shakes her head and then, after a second, points to the little girl with the ponytail.

"Just to your sister. Is that what you mean?"

Another nod.

"It is a bit weird, you know. Having a one-sided conversation."

Sunny shrugs, her face dropping a bit. I feel bad. I didn't mean to upset her. I want her to know that weird is all right in my book. The girls at school think I'm strange for being so obsessed with old movies.

"I don't mind," I add quickly. "The not-talking bit, I mean. I go quiet sometimes too. Flora's the chatterbox in our family. Flora's my mum. We live in Dublin. She's away travelling at the moment so I'm staying with Nan. Do you know Nan?"

Sunny nods.

"I'm feeling a bit homesick, to be honest. I don't know anyone here."

Sunny points to herself.

"You?"

She nods.

"You mean I know you? I guess I do."

Sunny picks up her sketchbook, flicks back a page and points to it. My own face is staring back at me – freckles, mad curls and all. Except it's not me in the picture – it's a girl dressed in a tunic and bratt, standing in front of a castle. Sunny scribbles a few words under the picture. "You belong here. Like Red Moll."

I look at Sunny and she looks back at me. At exactly the same moment, our faces break into two wide smiles.

Chapter 5

Before dinner I flick through some more of Granny Ellen's old photo albums with Nan. I'm trying to keep my mind off how strange and different Little Bird feels. Just as we sit down to eat, Nan's mobile starts to ring. It's the theme tune from *The Muppet Show*, which makes me smile. Mine's a boring piano riff. I should ask Nan where she got the *Muppet* music.

"Hello, Flora," she says. "Yes, of course. She's dying to talk to you… It's six in the evening here. We're just about to eat dinner, in fact… Not at all. I can pop her plate in the Aga." Nan smiles at me. "It's your mum. She's ringing from her stopover at Singapore. You can take it through to the living room if you like. I'm just handing over to Mollie now, Flora… Sorry? I didn't quite catch that." Nan's voice goes a little flat. "Really? What a shame. Why's that? … Oh, I see… Yes, of course she can… No, you should definitely tell her yourself… I'll put her on now. Have a safe flight, Flora. See you soon." She looks a little worried. What has Flora done now?

"You talk to your mum now, pet," she says, handing me

the phone. "I'll be right here waiting for you when you've finished."

Once I'm in the living room, I say, "Flora? Is everything all right? You haven't missed your flight, have you? Or lost your passport again?"

"Course not, Mopsy," Flora says. "I wouldn't have got on the flight without a passport now, would I? It was in the fruit bowl, like you said. Our Sydney flight's about to be called, but I have a few minutes to catch up with my favourite girl."

"How was your first flight?" I ask.

"Long. Very, very long. A whole thirteen hours. And the next bit is almost as long. But the film crew kept me entertained. They're all boys, but that doesn't bother me. They're pets and they're being so kind, carrying my bags and making sure I'm drinking enough water. Julian is obsessed with staying hydrated. He's the director. We chatted for hours on the plane, and then we watched the same movie at the exact same time – this funny old comedy called *Groundhog Day* – so we could both laugh together and not feel like idiots. Hang on a second… People are starting to stand up. I think they've just called our flight. Yep, the boys are waving at me. I'll see you very soon."

"In three weeks," I say.

"Must dash, darling. Be good for Nan now, won't you? Love you lots. Kiss, kiss." I can hear her lips smacking against the phone.

And then she's gone. I walk back into the kitchen.

Nan looks up from the table. "Are you all right, Mollie? Such a shame about Paris."

"What about Paris?"

Nan shifts awkwardly. "Didn't Flora tell you?"

"Tell me what?"

Her lips go so thin they almost disappear. "Oh, Flora," she murmurs.

"What's going on?" I'm starting to get a bad feeling.

"Sit down, child." Her voice has gone all low and serious.

"I don't want to sit down. What is it? Just tell me."

"I asked your mum to break the news to you herself. But clearly she didn't." Nan sighs deeply. "Her plans have changed, sweetheart. You can't go to Paris with her. She hadn't actually asked anyone about it until today. She talked to her director and he said the production company won't allow it. Something to do with their insurance. I'm sorry." Nan puts her hand on my arm, but I shake it off.

"No, you're not," I say. "You don't care about me. You've only just met me. I am going to Paris with Flora – she promised."

"I'm so sorry, child. I don't know what to say. Flora shouldn't have promised without checking first."

"You're a liar!" I say. "I know she's coming for me. And I'm not a child." I dash out of the kitchen, sprint out of the front door and keep running down the dark, muddy track until my lungs are bursting. At the end of the lane I turn left and run down the road, towards the harbour.

When the stitch in my stomach becomes unbearable, I

stop and bend over, sucking in big gulps of air. The worst thing is I know Nan is telling the truth. Flora's always doing daft things like this. I feel so let down.

"Are you sure no one minds me tagging along?" I'd asked her one evening when we were talking about what clothes I'd need for Paris.

"Why would they, Mollie Mops? It's not like you'll be any trouble. No, it's all hunky-dory," Flora had reassured me.

I never dreamed that she hadn't even asked them! How could she be so stupid?

Nan must think Flora's a right fool. And there was such pity in her eyes. Poor Mollie – nobody wants her. Not even her own flaky mum.

I crouch down at the side of the road, wrap my arms around my legs and press my eye sockets against my knees. I'm so angry and upset. When I've caught my breath, I stand up. It's creepy out here on my own. I'm sure I can hear rats or something scuttling in the hedgerows. It's cold too, and the only light is from the moon. Why aren't there any streetlights? Stupid island!

I know I'll have to go back to Nan's house eventually – I don't have any other option – but right now I can't face her. I shouldn't have shouted at her like that and run away. The Paris thing isn't her fault. I could go down to the cafe, but it's probably closed by now and, anyway, it's the first place Nan would look for me. There's a rusty old gate beside me that leads into a field. Past the field I can just make out a dark shape hidden in the trees. It's Red Moll's castle. The perfect place to hide.

I climb the gate and walk through the field, my Converse boots squelching on the wet grass. I clamber over a low wall and walk through the mossy old trees. The air smells of rotting wood and damp leaves. And then I stop. In front of me is Red Moll's castle. Or a bit of the castle – only one corner of the building is fully intact, but it's still really impressive. The two remaining walls are the height of a double-decker bus, the upper half covered with dark green ivy. There are small slit windows that were for archers to shoot through. We studied castles at school. The boys were fascinated by the "toilets" – holes in a stone seat with a sewage pit below. Boys are always interested in gross stuff like that.

I'm still fuming. Why is this happening to me? Why does Flora always let me down? I pick up a long stick from the ground and, in my anger, start hitting the wall, hard, making moss fly off it in gloopy lumps. Then I lash out at the ferns growing around the base of the castle, whacking them with such force that the leafy fingers are stripped from their stalks.

"What are you playing at?"

I jump and swing around, my heart racing in my chest. A boy steps out of the trees. He's wearing shorts, work boots and a hoodie. Shorts! It's February. Is he crazy?

"What are *you* playing at?" I shout back. "You nearly gave me a heart attack."

"Why are you hitting Red Moll's castle? That's a national monument, that is. Or at least it should be."

"It's been here for hundreds of years," I say. "It's not going to fall down just because I take a swipe at it. And Red Moll's hardly going to mind now, is she?"

"Her ghost might. And look at the mess you're making." He kicks at the tangle of moss and fern at my feet.

I start to feel guilty. He's right – it is a mess and I shouldn't have done it. I've made a mess of everything today, but I'm not going to tell him that. "I don't believe in ghosts," I lie. "And who made you Protector of the Ruins? Are you some sort of teenage security guard?"

"Don't be stupid."

"What are you doing up here then?"

"None of your business."

"Were you spying on me?"

"As if," he says. "You've missed the last ferry, you know."

"I'm not getting the ferry. I'm staying on this stupid hick island, worse luck."

He gives a sudden laugh. "You're Mollie Cinnamon."

I could kill Nan. Has she told absolutely everyone on Little Bird about me?

"You are, aren't you?" he says. "You know, your name makes you sound like a sweet or a cake. A cupcake from the Songbird Cafe!"

"I am *not* a cupcake!" I say.

"OK, OK. I was only joking."

"What's it matter to you who I am, anyway?"

"Nothing. Only Nan asked me and Lauren to look out for you on Monday in school, that's all. We're in the same class."

In the same class as Lauren? This can't be happening. "Is she your girlfriend or something?" I ask him.

"No! She's my twin sister. And I think she has it in for you. You might need to watch your back."

"Don't worry. I can look after myself."

"I can see that. But you can't bring your stick to school." The edges of his mouth are twitching, like he's trying not to grin.

"Why are you smiling at me like that?" I ask.

"No reason. I'll be seeing you around, Mollie 'Not a Cupcake' Cinnamon." He turns and strides back through the trees, hands in his pockets, whistling to himself.

I glare at his disappearing back. What an annoying boy! Who does he think he is, laughing at me? And I still can't believe he's in my class. With Lauren and probably that Chloe girl too. I let out a groan and throw my stick after him. It clatters off a tree trunk.

"Don't damage the trees as well, Mollie Cinnamon," he shouts back at me.

"Shut up," I mutter under my breath. "Leave me alone. All of you."

When I get back to Summer Cottage, I'm still feeling angry with the world. And tired. And lonely. And cold. Nan welcomes me and makes me hot chocolate as if I've just been out on a nice country walk. She doesn't say a word about my outburst, or Paris, or ask what I've been doing for the last half-hour, which is pretty decent of her. I guess she figures I feel rotten enough as it is, without going over it all again. She's right. I absolutely, one hundred per cent do not want to talk about it.

When I've finished my hot chocolate, she lets me take the laptop to my room to email Flora. I put "Paris!!!" in the subject line and then begin to type.

Dear Flora,

Nan told me the news. Can't you ask the TV people again about Paris? Maybe there's some special travel insurance you could get for me or something? I hate it here. Nan's nice, but there's nothing to do. You were right – it's really, really, really BORING.

I met some of the girls from my new school earlier and they're horrible. One of them has a horrible brother too. I'm not going to have any friends at school and I bet they'll all make fun of me.

Will you talk to the TV people, Flora, please? I'm begging you.

Don't leave me here.

Mollie XXX

I shut the lid of the laptop and fix my eyes on the photograph of Audrey Hepburn. She was sent to boarding school at five and her dad left the family when she was six. She didn't exactly have it easy either.

"Did you have a flaky mum too, Audrey?" I ask her smiling face.

The moon is shining in through my window and I get up to close the curtains. I stare outside for a moment, feeling utterly miserable. I can see the harbour and the roof of Alanna's cafe just below me. There's a tiny pinprick of light flying through the velvety sky just above the building. It's a shooting star!

"Make a wish, child," Granny Ellen told me once when we saw one. I make my second wish since I came to the island. But it's the same one. *Take me home, shooting star. Please take me home.*

A little later I'm in bed, trying to get to sleep, when I hear someone creep into my room.

"Mollie?" Nan whispers. "Are you awake?"

I don't want to talk to her, so I pretend to be asleep.

"May St Brigid keep you safe, child," she says softly. There's a slight rustling above my head and then she leaves the room, closing the door softly behind her.

I open my eyes and sit up. A sliver of moonlight is shining in through the crack between my curtains and I can just make out a tiny doll tied to the metal bedhead. The straw doll that grants wishes. I lie back down and press my head into the pillow. I'll need more than a straw doll to keep me safe, particularly with Lauren around. Weeks and weeks stuck here with no friends and nothing to do. I can't bear it.

Chapter 6

On Sunday afternoon I'm sitting in the alcove off the kitchen, flicking through one of Nan's cookery books. I didn't sleep well again last night. I had a dream about getting lost in a crowded airport. I was tiny and everyone else was huge. I asked for help, but no one could understand me. It was a very strange dream. I woke up at four and couldn't get back to sleep again, so I just lay there, tossing and turning.

"Hi, Mollie. Is Nan here?" I jump and the book clatters to the ground.

It's Alanna.

"Sorry, didn't mean to startle you." She bounces towards me and I can hardly take my eyes off her. She's wearing a moss-green jumper dress with a canary-yellow sleeveless puffa jacket thrown over the top. Her hair is tucked under a woolly Aran bobble hat. On anyone else the outfit would be ridiculous, but on Alanna it looks great.

"That's OK." I duck my head and pick up the book.

"Nice stripy mittens, by the way. Where did you get them?"

"My granny knitted them for me." I stroke the soft, fluffy

wool with my fingertips. They were my birthday present the year I turned eight. I loved them so much she made me a second pair in case I ever lost the first. They're fingerless, so I can wear them all the time, even indoors.

"Magic." Alanna leans over and reads the title of the book. *"The Hummingbird Bakery Cookbook."* She smiles. "Do you like baking?"

"Sometimes."

"Any time you'd like to help out in the cafe, you're more than welcome. Sunny works in the kitchen a couple of times a week. She's there now, in fact, with her mum. They're keeping an eye on the place for me. I can't pay much, but you can eat as many cupcakes as you like."

I'm suddenly shy and slightly in awe of her. "Thanks," I say. "I'll think about it. But isn't the cafe closing or something?"

"Where did you hear that?" Alanna's face has gone pale, making faint freckles on her cheeks stand out.

I shrug. I don't want to admit that I was eavesdropping on Alanna's conversation with Nan.

Luckily she doesn't push for an answer.

"Hopefully it won't come to that," she says. "I'm doing everything I can to keep it open. I took out a big loan to pay for the conservatory, you see, and I'm having trouble paying it back. But I will. I just need more time."

"Can't your mum and dad help?"

"No. They're … they're not around."

There's an awkward silence.

"Nan?" Alanna reminds me. "Is she here?"

"Oh, sorry, she's gone over to the Cotters' house to borrow one of Lauren's school skirts for me. I have to start at Bethlehem Heights tomorrow."

"I bet you're delighted about having to wear one of Lauren's hand-me-downs," Alanna says, rolling her eyes.

I laugh. "Tell me about it. Nan offered to buy me a uniform, but it would be a waste. I won't be here long."

"You're off to join your mum soon, aren't you? Paris, right?"

"Yes," I say firmly. "Paris."

"Well, you won't see Nan for a while if she's at the Cotters'. Nora, Lauren's mum, loves a good gossip. She has quite the sharp tongue, too. Lauren takes after her, unfortunately. But Landy's a pet. He's Lauren's twin brother. Have you met him yet?"

Landy. So that's what the boy from the castle is called. "I bumped into him last night." I don't tell her the details – running away from Nan's *and* getting caught hitting the castle by Landy – it's all too embarrassing.

"Stick with him tomorrow," she says. "And pay no attention to Lauren. Her bark's worse than her bite. Same with Chloe. Bonny's sweet. I just wish she didn't hang on Lauren's every word. Now I'd better get back to the cafe. Tell Nan I stopped by to drop this off." She pulls a brown envelope out of her pocket and places it on the desk. "Only a boring bank statement, I'm afraid." She gives a fake yawn. "Oh, and I nearly forgot. This is for you." She hands me a small dark blue bottle.

The glass is cool against my skin. "What is it?"

She smiles, her eyes all warm and kind. "Put a few drops on your pillow before you go to bed. It will help you sleep."

How does she know I've been having trouble sleeping?

"Does it really work?" I ask.

"My grandmother's remedies always work. Now, I have to skedaddle. Valentine's Day is only a hop and a skip away and I have primrose to pick for a potion. Don't be a stranger now, promise?"

After she's gone, the whole room seems flatter. I wish she was still here.

Curious, I twist the small gold cap off the bottle she gave me and sniff. I'm instantly hit by the scent of apples, lemon and freshly cut grass. I breathe in again, and it makes my nose tingle. I give a huge yawn. Maybe Alanna's strange potion really can help me sleep better. But it's probably just the power of suggestion. Another huge yawn makes my jaw crack and I put the cap back on. If only Alanna could make me another special remedy – to make me feel less lonely. But I guess that's impossible.

On Monday morning, I wish I'd taken Nan up on her offer to buy me a new school uniform. I'm sitting in the car in the hand-me-downs that Nan brought back from Lauren's yesterday. I'm not into minis, and this scratchy beetroot-coloured skirt is more like a belt. It's so short that the equally beetroot jumper almost covers it. I'm also wearing a white school shirt that's a bit too tight for me: one of Chloe's cast-offs. I've never worn a full uniform before – my current school has a dark green hoodie with a crest on it, but that's it – and it makes me feel strange and uncomfortable.

I've been to lots of different schools. Flora never likes to stay in one place for too long. Granny Ellen used to say she had "itchy feet". It means I have to leave friends behind and make new ones. I'm used to it by now, though. I remind myself that the first day is always horrible, but then it gets easier.

"Stop pulling at your skirt, Mollie," Nan says. "It'll be fine. All the girls wear them short, you've got nothing to worry about."

"Apart from my stick-insect legs," I say. "Thank goodness it's only for two months. And I have Paris to look forward to. As soon as Flora gets my email I'm sure she'll sort things out." I still haven't heard back from her, but maybe she's somewhere they don't have Internet or mobile reception. Or maybe she's too busy to answer me. I couldn't stop thinking about it yesterday. She has to make the TV people change their minds about Paris.

"I hope she does, child," Nan says. "But for now you'll be attending Bethlehem Heights, so best make the most of it. Better get going – the ferry's waiting. Shall I stay with you or—?"

"No, I'll be fine." I grab my rucksack from the footwell, open the passenger door and jump out.

"Don't forget your jacket, child," she calls.

I hear sniggers behind me. Lauren, Chloe and Bonny are

65

standing by the harbour wall, watching me. Nan was right – their skirts are almost non-existent.

"Hi, Nan," Lauren simpers. "Don't worry. We'll take good care of Mollie, won't we, girls?"

"Well then, I'll leave Mollie in your capable hands, Lauren," Nan says, getting out of the car and moving towards me as if she's about to give me a hug or something. I step away quickly and she gives me a wave before getting back into the car.

"Don't think I've forgotten what you said in the cafe," Lauren says as soon as Nan's gone. "It's not on, you know, slagging off the island. You think you're so cool just because you're from Dublin. Who cares about stupid Dublin? It's smelly and noisy, and Mum says most people in Dublin would move if they could."

"To New York or Paris," I say. "Not to a snoresville island in the middle of nowhere."

Lauren jabs a finger in my chest. "Just watch it, understand? There'll be no Nan or Alanna to look after you today."

I sit as far away as I can from Lauren and her cronies on the ferry. Unfortunately, that means sitting near Landy. He nods at me and says, "Hi, Mollie Cinnamon," with that annoyingly smug smile on his face again.

I scowl at him. The truth is, I'm feeling a bit shaken after what Lauren has just said to me.

"It's like that, is it, city girl?" he says, turning away. "I'm just trying to be friendly." He sticks his headphones over his ears, leans his head back against the cabin wall and closes his eyes.

While Lauren and Chloe are looking at something on Chloe's iPhone, Bonny shuffles along the red plastic seats to sit beside me.

"You all right?" she whispers. "Lauren didn't scare you, did she?"

"I'm fine."

"Don't mind her – she's jealous. She'd love to live in Dublin. And Landy's a good guy. He just likes winding people up."

"What are you doing over there, Bonny?" Lauren shouts across. "You need to see this giggling baby. It's so funny."

"See you later, Mollie." Bonny jumps up and rejoins Lauren and Chloe, leaving me all on my own again.

The teachers at Bethlehem Heights seem decent enough. The year head, Miss McKennedy, is also our science teacher, and she tries to make me feel welcome by finding me a place to sit beside Bonny. Landy's pretty much ignoring me. I can't really blame him after the way I behaved on the ferry. At least Bonny is friendly when Lauren and Chloe aren't around.

We have English and geography before morning break. I've done some of the work we're covering already, like how to write formal letters. Other things are new – oxbow lakes and other river stuff – but at least none of it is too hard. I keep thinking of what lessons I'd be doing back at home and wishing I was there. I'd be sitting beside Shannon and chatting when the teacher's back was turned.

"How are you finding things so far?" Bonny asks me as the class files outside to take soil samples for biology.

"All right, I guess," I say.

"Is it different to your school back home?"

I nod. "Mine's a lot bigger, for starters. We have four classes in every year, and it's a new building, so the classrooms are a lot brighter." Bethlehem Heights has mustard walls with flaky damp patches, and dark brown carpet tiles. Plus, all the windows are dripping with condensation.

"Lauren says your mum's on the telly. Is that true?" she asks. "Is she really famous?"

"There you are, Bonny." It's Lauren. Bonny immediately moves further away from me. "She's not famous," Lauren says. "She's only a weather girl. It's hardly Hollywood. Chloe, find that clip of Mollie's mum on YouTube. It's so funny."

I feel my cheeks heat up. I can guess which clip she means. Flora made one silly mistake, years ago – and, yes, I guess it is kind of funny – but trust them to find it!

Chloe holds up her iPhone and plays the video. In it, Flora mistakes the coast of Norway for Italy. It was one of her first days forecasting, she was very nervous and, to be honest, she's never been all that good at geography.

Bonny just laughs. "That is funny. And I recognize her – Flora Cinnamon, right?"

It gives me the confidence to say that Flora's presenting a travel show now.

"Oh, la-di-da," Lauren says. "A travel show – big deal."

I ignore her.

"You look like your mum," Bonny says. "You have the same eyes. It's just the hair that's different." She's right – our hair couldn't be more different. Flora's hair is poker-straight while mine is super wavy.

"You know what your hair reminds me of?" Lauren says. "Worms. Lots of wriggling red worms stuck on top of your head. Maybe we should call you Worm Head. Or Wormie." She upends a large stone with the tip of her shoe. Pale pink worms, woodlice and earwigs move away from the sudden light. Lauren picks up a worm. She holds it up to my face. I twist my head, but it hits my cheek and sticks for a second before falling off. I rub fiercely at my slightly sticky skin. Disgusting!

The rest of the day doesn't get any better. During maths, Lauren and Chloe flick pieces of chewed-up paper into my hair, and during Irish class they make fun of my accent. On the way back to the ferry I lag behind them, hoping they'll just leave me alone. Landy's following us, keeping his distance.

"Wormie can't go back to Dublin, you know," I hear Lauren say loudly so that I can hear. "Her mum's off filming and she doesn't want Mollie tying her down. Her dad isn't around and her granny's dead. Nan only took her in because she had to. No one wants her."

Bonny surprises me by standing up for me. "Poor Mollie,"

she says. "Maybe we should be nicer to her."

When Lauren and Chloe stare at her, Bonny says, "What? I'm just saying it must be hard."

She half-turns and blushes when she realizes I'm behind them. I know she's being kind, but I hate people feeling sorry for me, so I poke out my tongue. I regret it the second she turns away.

On the ferry, I listen to my iPod and stare out of the window, turning my music up high, so I don't have to deal with their teasing. I try to forget what Lauren said: *No one wants her*.

As we chug into the harbour, I spot Click leaping out of the waves, but even that doesn't cheer me up. Not today.

Chapter 7

Nan is standing at the harbour wall, waiting to meet the ferry. I can't deal with Lauren being all sweet and innocent in front of her after spending the day tormenting me, so I stay on the boat until everyone else has climbed off. I wait so long that the captain, a woman with windswept blonde hair and a tanned face, sticks her head into the cabin. "Are you coming back to the mainland with me? Or are you getting off?"

"Sorry." I make my way slowly towards the harbour steps.

"How was your first day?" Nan asks as soon as I reach her.

I stay quiet.

"That good, eh?" she says. "Let's get you home."

She tries to get me to talk all the way to Summer Cottage and again during dinner, but I don't feel like it.

"Listen, Mollie," she says after we've eaten. "I know first days can be difficult, but give it time. And I'm here if you want to talk, OK? I'm not going to force you, but you know what they say, 'A problem shared is a problem halved.'"

I nod silently.

"PJ was full of stories about the school he taught at. Lots of embarrassing things used to happen to the children. One girl wore her slippers to school by mistake – fluffy rabbit slippers – and a boy of twelve called the teacher 'Mum'. In fact, that used to happen a lot. Oh – and this is the worst one of all – a pair of pink knickers fell out of the bottom of a boy's tracksuit once when he was running. They were his sister's and they'd got mixed up with his uniform in the tumble-dryer."

I try not to laugh, but I can't help it. "Nan, that's terrible! Really?"

She nods and smiles. "I know – poor lad. He was mortified. It took him weeks to get over it. But none of it was as bad as what happened to me, of course. It still makes me cringe even now. It was truly awful."

"What happened?"

"Well, when I was a teenager at Bethlehem Heights, back in the days of the dinosaurs, we had to wear big nylon knickers for gym, instead of shorts."

I wrinkle up my nose. "Just knickers?"

"Yes, a white Aertex shirt tucked into big purple knickers." She shudders. "Horrible. Anyway, my mum had forgotten to buy me new gym knickers, so she found some white ones and dyed them purple instead. She boiled them with some beetroot from the garden. It worked like a charm. Until I wore them in our first gym lesson. It was September and we were outside – our gym teacher was obsessed with fresh air – and it started to rain really heavily. Guess what happened? Purple dye started running down my legs. Everyone was pointing at me and whispering. I was so embarrassed I started to cry. For the rest of my time at school I was known as Beetroot Girl. I know school can be awful sometimes, Mollie, but at least nothing like that happened, did it?"

"No. But they did make fun of me."

"I see. Try not to take it to heart, child. It will take them a few days to get to know you, that's all. Would you like to take the laptop up into your bedroom and see if Flora's emailed you back? Have you finished all your homework?"

I haven't even started, but obviously I don't admit that. "Thanks, Nan," I say, sidestepping her question.

I take Nan's laptop upstairs with me and click into my email account. There it is – a reply from Flora. Result! I open it, holding my breath.

All I want to read is: "Dear Mollie Mops, Nan has it all wrong. Of course you're coming to Paris with me…"

Sent: Monday 4 February 08:00
From: floracinnamon21@gmail.ie
To: molliemops@irelandmail.ie
Subject: I WANT TO MARRY MY HOTEL ;-)

Dear Mollie Mops,
I've only got a sec. Things are SO busy at the mo – you wouldn't believe it.

We arrived in Sydney yesterday afternoon (Sunday) and the weather is amazing – hot and sunny and 25 degrees. Not like rainy old Ireland.

There're four of us. Julian is the boss of Team Travelling Light – he's the director. Have I told you about him already? Anyway, he's super smart and funny. There's also Fintan the sound man (small and cuddly) and Lucas the cameraman (tall and a bit intense, but very sweet). The producer and the researchers are based in the Dublin office. They do all the practical stuff like booking flights and hotels.

It's hard work, but I'm learning LOADS. Julian is even helping me write some of my own scripts. Imagine – me, a scriptwriter! It's so exciting, Mopsy!!! And he's so handsome too. All wavy black hair and dark stubble – just like a Hollywood movie star.

Our hotel is called The Old Sydney Harbour Hotel and it's right on the water. It's super swish – all grey and silver and ultra chic. You should see the size of the white marble bathroom. The bath's so enormous you can practically swim in it, and standing under the huge shower is like being in the rainforest. (I'm so in love with the hotel I think I want to marry it! ;))

We're finishing off our scripts today and we start filming tomorrow. Our first stop is Bondi Beach for some serious swimming and body-surfing action. I can't wait.

I really wish you could join me while I'm filming in Paris, but it's just not possible. Julian said even if our insurance did allow it, it wouldn't be professional.

You do understand, don't you, poppet? We'll have a special girls' trip another time, I promise. And Nan's happy to look after you until I get back – less than eight weeks now. It'll fly by!

I'd better run, Mopsy. I think that's Julian banging on the door. We're supposed to be going for dinner together and I'm not even dressed – oops! You know what I'm like, darling, Johnny come late, late, lately!!!

Have to dash. Love you. XXX

Flora's not taking me to Paris. She's off having a brilliant time while I'm stuck here with Nan for two whole months. It's so unfair. Now I feel even worse. Lauren's right – nobody wants me.

I'm too upset to email Flora back so I ring Shannon, but there's no reply. Then I remember that she has hockey training on a Monday night. She's sent me a couple of "Miss you already" and "Wish you were here" text messages over the last few days, but it's not the same as talking to her.

There's a knock on the door. "Mollie, can I come in? I have some dessert for you." Nan walks in before I have a chance to answer. She puts a bowl down on the desk. Inside is apple crumble and it smells delicious. There's even a big dollop of whipped cream on top.

"Is there anything from Flora yet?"

"You were right – she's not coming for me. She's so disappointed, though. She really wanted to see Paris with me. I know she's missing me loads. She's kind of useless without me, actually. Always losing things and being late for appointments. I'm like her best friend." My voice breaks on the last word.

"I'm sure she misses you dreadfully, pet. I'm sorry. I know you must be sad about not going to Paris." She pats my arm. "I'm just going outside to feed the worms before it gets too dark, but you eat your dessert and after that I'll make you a nice mug of hot chocolate. How does that sound?"

"Worms? You keep pet worms?"

"I guess I do. I have a wormery in the garden full of tiger worms. Hungry fellows they are. They eat all kinds of kitchen waste: apple cores, potato peel – things like that. Hair and nail clippings too – anything organic."

"How big are they?"

"Huge, much larger than normal worms. Do you want to see them?"

Normally I'd go, "Euw, disgusting, no way," but instead I say, "Yeah, OK." Let's face it, I don't exactly have anything else to do. How sad is that? Then I remember what Lauren said earlier.

"They called me Worm Head today," I say. "They said my hair was like worms." Saying it out loud makes me feel all small and alone again.

"Who did?" Nan asks sharply.

I shrug. "Some of the girls at school."

Nan goes quiet for a moment. "Girls can be awfully mean sometimes. You have McCarthy hair, just like Red Moll's, and you should be proud of it. Pay no attention and hold your head up high. Don't let silly girls like that get to you."

"OK." Funnily enough, I feel a tiny bit better. Nan's right – Red Moll wouldn't be scared of the likes of Lauren Cotter. From now on I'm going to be like Red Moll and stick up for myself.

Chapter 8

On Tuesday morning I decide to walk down to the ferry alone. At least that way Lauren and Chloe can't laugh about Nan fussing over me and calling me "child".

"It's only down the road," I tell Nan.

"You have a point. And I guess you'd like to walk home on your own too?"

"Yes!"

"In that case I'll see you later."

"Bye, Nan." I rush towards the lane in case she changes her mind about joining me.

"You've forgotten your jacket, Mollie," she calls after me.

"I have a hoodie on."

I hear her mutter something about me catching my death, but I keep walking. When I reach the harbour, I spot Landy ahead of me, boarding the ferry, but there's no sign of Lauren and Chloe, or Bonny. I guess they make a habit of being late. There are white tips on the waves in the bay and the ferry is pulling on its ropes – like a dog on its lead, dying to be walked.

The captain's standing at the back of the ferry and as I

board carefully, clasping the railing when I step onto the bucking deck, she smiles at me. "Morning, Mollie. How are you today? We haven't been introduced yet. I'm Mattie Finn."

"Hi." I don't ask how she knows my name. I'm getting used to everyone on the island knowing who I am. She offers me a hand to steady me, but I don't take it. I'll manage on my own, even if I do stumble a little.

"The sea's a bit choppy today, I'm afraid," she says. "Be careful."

I manage to get down the three steps and safely into the cabin. Landy's already there, sprawled in a seat, his long legs sticking out in front of him. "You'll need your sea legs today," he says.

I have no idea what he's talking about so I just nod at him and say, "Hi."

I hear Lauren before I see her.

"It's too windy for the ferry, Mattie," she moans. "We should get a day off."

"I'll be the judge of that, Lauren," Mattie tells her. "It's due to blow out later and stay calm for days. You're in luck. I think you'll make it to school every day this week."

"Great!" Lauren mutters. She spots me as she comes into the cabin. "Look, it's Wormie."

"Leave her alone, Lauren," Bonny says, her voice wavering a little and her face turning bright red. She looks scared but determined. I can't believe she's sticking up for me after I poked my tongue out at her yesterday. I give her a grateful smile.

"Have you gone crazy, Bonny?" Lauren says. "She thinks the island is a boring old dump." Her eyes narrow. "And guess what she told me in French class?"

"What?" Bonny asks.

What is Lauren talking about? I had to sit beside her in French class, worse luck, but I didn't say a word to her about anything, especially not Bonny. But the truth doesn't seem to matter to Lauren.

"We had a great old chat, in fact," she says. "Nan had told her about your dad running off with that Swedish tourist, Bonny. That's the only reason she's being nice to you – she feels sorry for you."

Bonny's face goes white and she looks like she's about to cry.

"Liar!" I say. "Nan didn't say anything about your dad, Bonny. I swear."

But Lauren is on a roll. "Come on, Wormie, you even told me about your own dad running off to Boston."

I stare at her, my mouth open. How can she make up such whoppers? She's despicable.

"I didn't tell her that either," I say to Bonny. "She's making it all up." I look at Lauren. "And it's completely different. My dad didn't run off to Boston, Lauren. He's *from* Boston. He was only in Dublin on holidays. It all happened before I was born, obviously, so it didn't have anything to do with me."

As soon as the words are out of my mouth, I know I've made it sound worse – as if in some way it was Bonny's fault that her dad left. Bonny looks hurt. She turns away from me.

"I'm sorry, Bonny. That came out wrong," I say.

"It's fine," Bonny murmurs, her eyes not meeting mine.

I swallow, feeling desperate. What can I say to make her believe me? "Tell her," I urge Lauren. "Go on – admit you made all that up."

Lauren just rolls her eyes at me. "You're going to have to face it, Wormie. No one likes you. Not even Bonny, and she likes everyone."

I struggle through the morning lessons feeling sad and lonely. I hate Lauren. She's such a liar. And poor Bonny. I can't believe her dad ran off like that. It must have been terrible.

After lunch we have science with Miss McKennedy. We have to go outside to take more soil samples – yawn. I lag behind the class, willing this horrible day to be over.

Lauren drops back to join me. "You think you're better than everyone, don't you, Wormie? The cool Dublin girl with the cool clothes and the cool mum on the telly. Funny, isn't it, that your mum presents a travel show? She can't be very bright, getting Norway and Italy muddled up like that. She'll probably get lost." She makes her voice all giggly and breathless. "Ooh, I'm in Paris. Look at the lovely Eiffel Tower. Oopsy! Sorry, it's actually the Spire in Dublin. Silly me."

"My mum is filming in Sydney right now," I say angrily. "And she managed to get there just fine. Keep your mouth shut in future. And stop calling me Wormie."

"Or what?" Lauren shoves me backwards, hard. I grab at her to stop myself from falling, but instead I manage to pull her down with me. I land on my bum, but she lands on her side and her cheek hits the ground. She gives an almighty wail.

"Miss! Miss! Mollie pushed me!" she yells. "I think she's broken my cheekbone. It hurts. Ow! Ow! Ow!"

"You pushed me," I say. "You're such a big fat liar."

Miss McKennedy is standing in front of us, her face purple with rage. "What on earth is going on? Get up, both of you."

Everyone is staring at me like I'm some sort of alien.

"She pushed me, Miss," Lauren wails. "I think I'm bleeding."

Miss McKennedy studies Lauren's cheek. It's flaming red, but there's no blood. "You're not bleeding, Lauren," she says. "Please stop wailing. Chloe, take Lauren to see the school nurse for an ice pack. Mollie Cinnamon, I'm taking you straight to the head's office, young lady. And I don't want to hear a peep out of you until we get there. Understand? Violence will not be tolerated at Bethlehem Heights."

"But that's so unfair, Miss," I protest. "Lauren started it. She said things about my mum and then *she* pushed *me*!"

"Not another word, Mollie. I mean it."

Miss McKennedy marches me up the corridor, holding me by the arm. She has quite a grip. I can't believe I'm the one in trouble. This is all so wrong. Lauren's the biggest liar ever. She should be here, not me.

Miss McKennedy and the head teacher, Mrs Joseph, talk

for a few minutes while I sit outside the office, my heart pounding. The school secretary gives me a few stern looks but otherwise ignores me.

Then the door opens and Mrs Joseph says, "Mollie, into my office, please."

My hands are shaking with nerves and my breath is catching in my throat. I feel like everything is brighter, louder, more intense. Mrs Joseph dismisses Miss McKennedy and shuts the door behind us, indicating where I should sit.

Mrs Joseph is wearing a red wrap dress, glasses with thick black frames and a frown you could plant potatoes in. She sits down behind a large mahogany desk, leans her elbows on the top and folds her hands together.

"This is a very bad start to your time at Bethlehem Heights, Mollie," she says. "Your great-grandmother will be very disappointed in you. I know girls can often say unkind things to each other, but you must come and tell us if that happens, not take matters into your own hands. We don't tolerate any kind of physical violence or bullying here."

Me? I'm not the bully! Before I can stop myself, I give a shocked laugh.

"Wipe that smile off your face, Mollie Cinnamon," she snaps. "This is no laughing matter. I've phoned the nurse and she says Lauren will be fine, but her cheek is badly bruised. Count yourself lucky you didn't give her concussion or worse. Now, this is something we must take very seriously indeed. Do you have anything to say for yourself?"

I sit there, my mind racing. I could try to explain what really happened, but no one's going to believe me.

When I don't respond, she goes on, "Why did you push Lauren? Did she say something to you?"

Lauren is such a good liar she's managed to turn everyone against me, even Bonny. No one will believe anything I say. I've had enough of Lauren and everyone at Bethlehem Heights, so I simply say, "I don't know."

Mrs Joseph looks at me for a second, then sighs and shakes her head. "I'm sorry, Mollie, but in that case I have no choice. You're suspended."

Chapter 9

I get the early ferry back to the island, which is a relief. Before I left school, I talked to Nan briefly on the phone and she sounded shocked and upset.

"We'll go over this properly when you get home," she said. "I've spoken to Mrs Joseph and we've agreed that a week's suspension is appropriate. And obviously you'll have to apologize to Lauren."

During the whole journey back, I feel like a rubber band that's been stretched and stretched to the limit. It's so unfair because I'm not a bully! This is all Lauren's fault.

When we reach Little Bird, Nan is waiting for me at the harbour wall. Her face is rigid, like stone. I feel sick. Maybe she'll send me away. And if Flora can't come back for me, what will happen? Will I have to stay in a children's home or with a foster family or something?

Once again I linger in the cabin until everyone else has got off.

"You all right, Mollie?" Mattie asks, sticking her head through the doorway. "Time to get off now."

I press my lips together and nod. But I'm not all right at all.

Mattie lowers her voice. "I've heard what Lauren's been saying to you on the ferry and it's not right. I'm not surprised you snapped." I must look confused because she adds, "I didn't like to say anything when you got on the ferry, but I'm afraid everyone knows about what happened at school. Lauren rang her mum from the nurse's office and news spreads fast on the island." She smiles at me reassuringly. "Not everyone is taken in by Lauren Cotter. Just tell Nan the truth."

My stomach is turning nervous somersaults as I step off the ferry and walk towards Nan. But when I reach her, she just sighs.

"Oh, Mollie, what am I going to do with you?" she says. "I need a strong coffee. Let's grab a drink at Alanna's before we head home and sort out all this mess."

"OK," I reply. Delaying things sounds like a good idea.

"Hi, Nan. Hi, Mollie," Alanna greets us as we walk into the cafe. "What can I get you both? Your usual?"

Nan nods. "Thanks, Alanna."

I can tell Alanna knows about the Lauren incident from the gentle smile she gives me. Mattie was right – news travels fast on Little Bird. My eyes start to sting with tears. Everyone must think I'm a terrible person. And I still can't believe Lauren said such horrible things about Flora. I know Flora can be a bit ditzy sometimes, but she's my mum. And she's funny and smart in her own way. She's also brilliant with people. "Flora, you could charm the bees." That's what Granny Ellen always told her.

"Don't look so frightened, child. I'm not going to eat you," Nan says. "I want you to tell me exactly what Lauren has been up to. I know a lot of people think that butter wouldn't melt in that girl's mouth, but I'm certainly not one of them and neither is Alanna. Mrs Joseph told me Lauren's side of the story. Now I want to hear your side."

"You're not sending me away?"

"Of course not! Is that what you've been thinking? Mollie, we're family, and family sticks together. No matter how near your cloak is, your flesh is always nearer."

Granny Ellen used to say that too. She said it was one of Red Moll's expressions. I'm so relieved that hot tears start to roll down my cheeks. I wipe them away, embarrassed. I hate people seeing me cry.

"Lauren was saying horrible things about Flora," I say in a rush. "I told her to stop and she pushed me. I grabbed her to stop myself falling and pulled her down too. And then she lied to everyone about what had happened. It wasn't my fault, you have to believe me."

"I do believe you, child. Come here." Nan gives me a big hug. And for the first time, I let her hold me, although I don't hug her back. She smells of baking and flowery perfume. It reminds me of Granny Ellen. It's like coming home.

"Lauren's the one who was nasty about your hair, isn't she?" Nan asks after a moment.

"Yes. And she said you didn't want me here. That no one wants me."

"Well, she couldn't be more wrong about that. I love you, Mollie. Of course I want you here." Nan pulls back a bit and looks at me. "From now on, if Lauren says anything unkind, come straight to me. Understand? I'd like to give her a piece of my mind. Her mother too."

"Don't, Nan, please. I can look after myself."

"You're just like my Ellen, and Red Moll before her, trying to battle the whole world by yourself. You don't have to fight alone, Mollie. Even Red Moll had supporters. We may not be a whole army, but you have me, and Alanna too. Don't be afraid to ask for help. Lauren can tell all the lies she wants," Nan says. "We're on your side, no matter what." She pulls me towards her again and squeezes me tight. This time I hug her back.

"Do I have to go back to that school?" I ask once I've pulled away. "Lauren's turned everyone against me and I don't have any friends. Even Bonny hates me. Can't I stay here with you instead?"

Nan brushes a curl off my face. "And do what, child?"

"My schoolwork. I have most of my textbooks with me. I could do essays and stuff until Flora's back."

Nan thinks for a second. "I suppose it might work. Let me talk to your school in Dublin and see what they think. And I'll need to discuss it with your mum, of course."

"Thanks, Nan." I'm starting to feel a little brighter. Nan

really does want me with her after all.

"And, Mollie, one last thing. I don't care what Mrs Joseph said – there's no way you're apologizing to Lauren. Just keep out of her way, understand?"

"Got it." There's no way I'm going anywhere near Lauren Cotter and her poisonous tongue ever again.

Chapter 10

The thing about not going to school is that routine goes out of the window. Personally I think that's a good thing – routine is so boring – but Nan doesn't see it that way. She's not impressed with all my lie-ins. I've had no problem with bad dreams since Alanna gave me that herbal remedy. I've been putting a few drops on my pillow every night and sleeping like a baby.

At ten on Thursday morning Nan marches into my room and whips open the curtains.

"Wakey-wakey, sleepy head," she says. "That's quite enough lazing around for you."

I groan. "Go away, Nan. Just give me a few more minutes."

"That's what you said at eight o'clock and again at nine. You had a day off yesterday and now it's time to get moving. Hard work and good care take the head off bad luck."

I sit up and rub my eyes. Hard work and good what? Nan's sayings make no sense when you've just woken up. "Nan, can I have one more day off, please? I'm tired."

"You're twelve, Mollie. How can you be tired? Now come

on – rise and shine. I have a heap of chores for you. And on Monday you'll be back to normal school hours. So there'll be no more lying-in during the week."

Nan talked to my school in Dublin yesterday. Most of my teachers agreed to email me work to do at home so that I won't fall behind. Flora was a little harder to get hold of. She wasn't answering her mobile, so Nan had to ring the production company in Dublin and they managed to track her down via Lucas, the cameraman, the only one of the team who actually answered his phone. She finally got to talk to Flora yesterday evening, and now it's official – I can study at Nan's house until Flora comes back to get me.

I'm so happy, but I hadn't realized I'd still have to get up early. "Great," I mutter, disappointed at the thought of no more lie-ins.

"You can always go back to Bethlehem Heights if you like."

"No way! Thanks for arranging everything, Nan."

"You're welcome, child. It will be nice to have you around the place more. But it's not an excuse to mess around, OK?"

"I know."

"Good. Now, get yourself dressed and we'll talk about the extra bits you're going to do every day in lieu of sports and things like that. Mollie, welcome to the world of work."

I stare at her. "I can't work. It's illegal – I'm too young. You'll get arrested or something."

Nan chuckles. "In case you haven't noticed, there are no guards on the island. And a few chores never killed anyone.

Now come on – the worms are waiting to be fed. That's number one on your job list."

After breakfast and feeding the worms – and, boy, do the rotting banana skins and potato peelings stink – Nan makes me sit down at the kitchen table and read the list she and Alanna have put together of things I can do on top of my schoolwork:

Mollie's Job List
1. Feed the worms.
2. Help Alanna in the cafe.
3. Keep a diary of your time on the island.

"Do I really have to keep a diary?" I ask. "I hate writing essays."

"What would you suggest doing instead?"

"I could watch movies and review them?"

Nan shakes her head and smiles. "Nice try, Mollie. But your movie suggestion gives me an idea. Wait there."

She comes back a few minutes later holding a small box, which she hands to me. Inside is a camera. It looks a few years old, but it's a good one.

"I promised you could use this, remember?" she says. "If you stay on top of all your English assignments, you can make a video diary instead of a written one."

"A video diary sounds OK," I say, still studying the camera. "It's actually called a vlog." In fact, I'm itching to get started.

I've always wanted a good camera, but Flora won't buy me one. She says they're too expensive and that I'll only drop it.

"Good. The camera's all yours. Now go on, have a play with it. There's no time like the present. The island awaits."

I turn the camera over carefully in my hands. For something so compact, it's surprisingly heavy. "Thanks, Nan," I say. "Oscars, here I come."

I pack my rucksack with some essentials – notebook, pen, water – and throw it over my shoulder. Nan gave me the notebook. It's a small black one with an elastic band around it to keep it shut. She said it was called a Moleskine notebook and that lots of creative people like writers and film-makers use them.

As I'm leaving, Nan takes two large oat biscuits from a jar in the cupboard and wraps them in tinfoil. "Here. In case you get hungry. It's a fine day – make the most of the light."

"I will. Thanks, Nan." I smile at her.

She smiles back. "It's nice to see you looking so happy for a change. You have a beautiful smile, Mollie."

As I walk down the lane, I think about Nan. She's being really kind to me. She said I needed a quiet day yesterday so she let me have a big long lie-in. She brought me breakfast in bed and I lazed under my duvet until lunchtime, reading my movie-star book. In the afternoon it was really rainy, so we had a movie marathon and ate home-made popcorn. It was actually really good fun. We watched *The Wizard of Oz* (my choice) and then *The Sound of Music* (her choice), and finally

Back to the Future after dinner (Nan suggested it and it was really good).

I guess I'm starting to get used to Nan and the island now. But I know I shouldn't get too settled here. When Flora finishes filming, it will be back to my old life again. I hope Shannon won't find a new best friend before I get home. She's sounded really busy in the few texts she's sent me, but then that's nothing new. Shannon does more after-school activities than anyone I know.

Suddenly, a small brown bird flies across the lane and lands in the mud in front of me. It's unusual looking, with black-and-white stripes on its head. I quickly turn on the camera and start to film him. As if he knows what I'm up to, he looks at me and starts chirping, his eyes sparkling in the sunlight. After a few seconds the bird flies away, but it's a good start to my vlog: "A Diary of Little Bird Island: Day One." A little bird on Little Bird – get it? I take out my Moleskine and write down some ideas for filming: "Island nature – birds, butterflies, insects". Then I remember Click and jot down "Marine animals – fish and mammals", which makes me think of the islanders – the people who live here now and famous islanders of the past.

That will be the hardest bit – people. I don't exactly have many friends here apart from Alanna and Sunny, and I can hardly interview Sunny. Red Moll is the only famous islander I know of and interviewing her will also be rather difficult, unless her ghost appears! I'll start with nature.

I walk on, keeping my eyes peeled for more birds. At the end of the lane I turn left, towards the harbour, and spy the same little bird again. He's hopping along the top of the bush beside me.

"That's a white-crowned sparrow," a voice says.

Landy is strolling down the lane towards me. I instantly feel my cheeks hotting up. He's one of the last people on earth I want to see right now.

"They're pretty rare," he adds when he reaches me. "Easy to spot with the zebra stripes."

"You frightened him away," I say angrily, to hide my embarrassment. "And what are you, some sort of bird expert?"

"No, but my dad's a twitcher."

"A what?"

"A birdwatcher. When he's not working on the campsite or building things."

"Shouldn't you be in school?" I ask.

"I didn't feel great this morning, but I'm OK now, so I'm going down to Alanna's to help Dad. He's a builder. He's fixing up some of the cafe windows for her. Why are you filming birds?"

"I just am. Can't you all leave me alone? I'm sorry I'm not from here, OK? But I haven't done anything wrong, whatever Lauren says."

Landy looks at me for a second, as if weighing something up. "Did you really push her?"

"No! I told her to stop being mean about my mum and

then she pushed *me*. I grabbed her to stop myself falling. It was an accident."

"I knew there was something odd about her story. Mum swallowed it, but I'm well used to my darling sister's lies. She's always getting me into trouble at home. Drives me mad." He looks down and kicks a stone into the bushes. "Hey, I'm sorry about the whole Bonny thing. I told her you didn't say anything about her dad. I was sitting right behind you and Lauren in French and I know you didn't say a word to Lauren."

"Did Bonny believe you?"

"I think so. And I told my folks about Lauren picking on you. She's not exactly speaking to me at the moment."

"You must be devastated," I say. "What a loss."

He grins. "Yeah, I know."

"Why are you being so nice to me?"

"It's about time someone stood up to Lauren. She gets away with murder."

"Do your parents always believe her?"

"Mum usually takes her side, all right, but Dad sees through her sometimes." He shrugs. "Hey, that's families for you, right?"

"Sure," I say, although to be honest, I don't know all that much about family dynamics as it's just me and Flora.

"Anyway, you never answered my question," he says. "What's with the camera?"

"I'm making a short movie about the island."

"Cool. I like movies."

"Let me guess. Action and adventure movies. James Bond. Car chases and guns."

"Sure. But I watch other things too."

"Favourite film?"

"Is this a test?"

"Maybe."

He thinks for a second. *"The Empire Strikes Back."*

I try not to look impressed. It's definitely the best of the *Star Wars* movies – dark and moody. It's the one where Luke finds out who his father really is.

"Yours?" he asks.

"Honestly?"

He tilts his head. "It can't be that bad."

"It's *The Wizard of Oz*," I admit.

He gives that annoying knowing smile of his.

"What?" I demand.

"Nothing. So is this movie you're making a musical with dancing scarecrows and flying monkeys?"

"Ha ha. Very funny."

Our conversation is interrupted by a loud rumbling noise.

"What is that?" I ask, alarmed.

"Dad," Landy says simply.

I start to feel nervous. I know Landy said his dad sees through Lauren sometimes, but she's still his daughter. As if reading my thoughts, Landy says, "Don't worry. I'll have a word with him about the Lauren thing."

Just then, a mud-splattered navy Land Rover jeep appears on the road, beeps its horn and pulls up beside us. A man with long sandy-brown hair tied back in a ponytail is sitting behind the wheel. He has Landy's pale grey eyes.

"Do you want a lift to Alanna's?" Landy's dad asks him through the open window.

"Sure," Landy says. He turns to me. "Would you like to come with us? You could help us sand down the windows."

"OK." Helping at the cafe is on my job list after all.

"Is that all right, Dad?" Landy asks him. "Can Mollie join us?"

The man looks at me for a long second. "Are you Mollie Cinnamon?" he asks me. "Nan's girl?"

I nod nervously.

Landy leans in through the window to talk to his dad, and I stand back. After a while the man nods at Landy and looks over at me. He smiles this time.

"Let's start again, Mollie," he says. "I'm Bat Cotter, Landy's old man. I have no idea what went on in school, but from what Landy's saying Lauren was to blame. Is that right?"

I think about my answer for a second. I may not like Lauren, but I'm no telltale.

"It was both our faults," I say. "We had a bit of an argument and it got out of hand."

"Are you sure?" he asks.

I nod firmly. "Yes."

"Fair enough. Thanks for telling me the truth. And you're

welcome to join us. Landy's right – we could do with another pair of hands."

Landy is staring at me, but I avoid his gaze.

"Want to ride on top, Mollie?" Bat says, jabbing his thumb towards the roof of the jeep. There's a framework of bars up there, like a large roof rack. "Great way to see the island."

"Isn't that a bit dangerous?" I ask.

"Don't be such a chicken," Landy says. "This old jeep doesn't exactly go very fast and we're only going down the road. It'll be fun."

Landy climbs up the small ladder attached to the back of the Land Rover as if he's been doing it his whole life, which he probably has. He hangs over the roof bars and offers me his hand.

"Come on, Mollser," he says. "It's just a ladder."

I'm about to frown at him for calling me that, but then I realize I quite like it. "A very small ladder," I point out. I hold onto the bars of the ladder and slowly make my way up towards him. Near the top, I take his hand and he helps me onto the roof. He's really strong.

"You need to sit down there, on one of the bars," Landy says. "Don't sit on the roof. It'll buckle. I'll sit close behind you, just in case."

I nod and do as he says. He crouches down behind me, which makes me feel safer.

"Ready up there?" Bat shouts out of his window. "You looking after Mollie, Landy?"

"Yes, sir!" Landy shouts back and he bangs twice on the roof of the jeep. And then we're off. At first I'm terrified. The Land Rover judders over potholes in the lane, lurching from side to side, and I hold on for dear life, my whole body tense with fright. I watch out for dips in the lane so I can be ready. But after a few minutes, I start to get used to the rhythm and I allow myself to look around.

I can see over all the hedges and past the patchwork of green fields towards the petrol-blue sea of Dolphin Bay. It's stunning, like a photo you'd see on a postcard. I hadn't realized how beautiful the island is until now.

"Whee!" I cry, as the air rushes past me. I arch my back and pretend to be a bird. "I'm flying!"

Everything seems to freeze in brilliant technicolour and there's just me and this gorgeous landscape and the wind blowing in my face. And I wouldn't be anywhere else in the whole wide world.

"You didn't have to say that to Dad – about it being partly your fault." Landy stops sandpapering the cafe's window frame and looks at me. "Lauren wouldn't have done that for you, you know. You're a very interesting girl, Mollie Cinnamon."

"Thank you. I think." I'm not quite sure what he means by "interesting", but I hope it's a compliment.

"How are you and Nan getting on?" he asks.

I fiddle with my piece of sandpaper for a second, finding a fresh corner that isn't covered in paint. Landy showed me how to rub the paper along the grain, taking the rough old bits of colour off the window jamb, so that his dad can paint them. Alanna was thrilled that I'd come to help. She gave me a huge smile, which made me feel really light inside.

"We're actually getting on pretty well," I say. And it's true – we really are. "Telling her about, you know, the school stuff helped a lot."

Landy's eyes go dark grey, like a stormy sky. "If Lauren says anything to you again, tell me about it, OK? I know you don't need my help, but just in case."

"Thanks." I smile to myself. I think I've made a new friend. Shannon will tease me about being friends with a boy, but that's all right. I don't feel so lonely any more. Maybe things aren't so bad after all.

Chapter 11

When I get back to Summer Cottage, I'm dying to email Flora and tell her all about Landy and the cafe and the fun I had helping out today. I took some footage of Landy and Bat standing on the jeep, painting the top of the window frames. When they realized I was filming them, they both started doing this really silly dance, swaying from side to side and doing crazy air guitar and leg kicks. Bat was laughing so much he nearly fell off the jeep.

After dinner I go upstairs with the laptop. There's an email waiting for me from Flora.

Sent: Wednesday 6 February 23:06
From: floracinnamon21@gmail.ie
To: molliemops@irelandmail.ie
Subject: Exciting news about NEWS!

Dear Mollie Mops,
I miss you so much, my darling. I can't wait to see you again. I wish you were here with me. I'd love to show

you all the cool things I've seen. I'm having SO much fun!

Today we climbed the Sydney Harbour Bridge. We had to go up ladders and catwalks, and I did a short piece to camera from the very top of the bridge – although it was pretty windy up there and I'm not sure how much you'll be able to hear. Just as well I'm not afraid of heights, unlike Fintan, the sound man. He froze halfway up one of the ladders until Lucas talked him down again. Julian had to take over the sound equipment. Luckily he doesn't mind heights at all. He loves danger. He's been skydiving and everything. He's offered to take me one day – which would be amazing! You'll adore Julian, Mopsy. He's wonderfully funny and so interesting. He knows loads of rock stars and models. He's even promised to introduce me to Bono – imagine!

Tomorrow we're off to Ku-ring-gai Chase National Park to check out some Aboriginal rock engravings of sharks and whales. Then once it's dark we're heading to Centennial Park to film golden brushtail possums – they're very rare and they only come out at night. Cool, eh?

And of course we have to film the Sydney Opera House. The building is just as amazing as it looks in photographs – like the huge white petals of some exotic flower opening up. Apparently the guy who designed it, Jørn Utzon, thought of the roof design while he was peeling an orange. They do look like the segments of an orange, all right.

Anyway, enough about me. Nan told me about what was going on at school and I'm sorry that one of the girls was picking on you. It's probably best that you don't go back. But do keep up with your studies. You're so bright, Mollie Mops, and I don't want you to fall behind.

I hope you're settling in with Nan on Little Bird. I know the islanders can be funny sometimes. They tend to stick together and can be suspicious of new people, especially amazingly cool, smart girls like you. Don't take it personally. I haven't been there for years, but I do remember what it was like – everyone knowing each other's business.

The time will fly, my darling. Before you know it you'll be back home with me. And I really can't wait. Until then, just hang in there, OK? I'll see you again very soon.

I almost forgot – there's been a slight change of plan. They're shortening our New Zealand trip by three days and we're flying back to Europe early. The producers want us to be in Paris for Valentine's Day next week. We've been asked to film a piece for "Six One News" and I'm going to present it. Me – on the news! Not doing the weather after the news – actually on the news!!! Mopsy, you have no idea how much this means to me. All those clever clogs newsreaders can't look down their snooty noses at me any more. I'm one of them. I just hope I don't fall into the river or something daft. :-)

I'm going to interview lovers snapping their locks onto one of the lock bridges. That was my idea, Mopsy. Julian had never even heard of the lock bridges. I told him he was such an old dinosaur.

Anyway, must run. We have so much filming to squeeze in over the next few days, it's unbelievable. We're flying to Auckland this Thursday for a whistle-stop tour of the city and from then on it's dash, dash, dash. So, unless there's an emergency, I won't be in contact. My poor old brain won't know what time of the day or night it is. After Paris it's straight back to Dublin for three days to do some editing and voice-overs (so sorry I won't make it down to see you, but it will be Manic Monday, my darling) and then we fly on to Rome and then New York, New York – so good they named it twice. The Big Apple of my dreams. Speaking of which – sweet dreams, my darling, darling Mopsy.

Good night, or "buonanotte", as they say in Paris.

I love you so much, Mollie Mops. I LOVE YOU, LOVE YOU, LOVE YOU.

Flora

XXXXXXXXXXXXXXXXXXXXXXXXXXXXXXXXXXXXXXXXXXXX
XXXXXXXXXXXXXXXXXXXXXXXXXXXXXXXXXXXXXXXXXXXX
XXXXXXXXXXXXXXXXXXXXXXXXXXXXXXXXXXXXXXXXXXXX
XXXXXXXXXXX + a billion trillion zillion

"*Bonne nuit,*" I whisper to myself. "It's *bonne nuit*, Flora. *Buonanotte* is Italian."

Reading Flora's email has made me feel totally miserable again. It sounds like she's having such an incredible time and I bet she's not missing me at all. And secondly, she's off to Paris without me. I was the one who told her about the lock bridges. Now she's going to share my discovery with the whole of Ireland and take all the credit. Everything seems so unfair and so wrong. We were supposed to visit the bridges together. And worst of all, she's going to be in Dublin, but she's not even bothering to come and see me. It's only a few hours' drive. If she really missed me as much as she claims, surely she'd jump in a car and visit me.

I wanted to tell her *my* news, but now I feel like a deflated balloon and I can't be bothered. I snap the lid of the laptop shut and stare at the photograph of Audrey Hepburn and her cat. "What was your mum like?" I ask her. "Did she drive you crazy?"

I love Flora, but sometimes she makes me want to scream.

Chapter 12

Alanna's sleep remedy didn't do me much good on Thursday night. I tossed and turned all night, thinking about Flora's email. I stay in my room for most of Friday and pretend to be doing my schoolwork, but mainly I just stare out of the window and doodle in my notebook.

On Saturday morning I'm sitting at the kitchen table, moving my cereal around my bowl, still thinking about Flora. I haven't replied to her email yet. Should I beg her to come and visit me? Or should I try to forget that my own mum isn't all that interested in seeing me?

Nan slides me a glass of orange juice. "Alanna was wondering if you'd like to help out in the cafe today."

"I don't really feel like it."

"What's up, pet?" Nan says. "You seem a bit out of sorts this morning. And you were the same yesterday."

Nan's face is soft and kind, like Granny Ellen's. As I look at her and think how nice she is, I get a sudden burst of inspiration. "Can you drive me up to Dublin, Nan? To see Flora. She said in her last email that she's going to be back for three days, just after Valentine's Day. I'm not sure about the exact date, but I can ask her. Maybe we could drive up and surprise her." It's the perfect plan. We can just appear and go, "Ta-da!" That way she'll have to act all happy to see me, even if she isn't.

Nan looks worried. Eventually she says, "I'm not sure surprising your mum would be such a great idea."

"Why not?"

"It's … complicated. Maybe you could ring when she's home and have a good long chat?"

"You can't give someone a hug on the phone. And why is it complicated?"

"You'll have to ask your mum."

"Ask her what?"

Nan looks awkward. She stays quiet.

"I'm sick of this stupid family," I say. "I've got a right to know what's going on. Flora hates having difficult conversations. She's always been like that. She won't let me talk about Dad or about Granny Ellen. And you're just the same."

Nan's face colours a little. "That's not fair. It's not my news to tell, Mollie."

"So you're not going to tell me what's happening?"

"It's nothing bad, I promise."

"Then what is it, Nan. Please?"

Nan sighs. "Flora has a new boyfriend, that's all. She didn't want to tell you while she was away and until she knows if it's serious. They'll be staying at the Merrion Hotel when they're back in Dublin. A post-Valentine's Day treat, apparently. She told me so that I'd know how to get hold of her if I needed to."

Suddenly it all starts to make sense. "So instead of coming to see me, she's staying in some posh hotel? With Julian, the director guy? Is that right?"

"Did she tell you about him?" Nan asks, surprised.

"Not that he's her boyfriend. But she's always going on about him in her emails."

"She does seem very keen on him. I'm not sure she's thinking straight at the moment."

"She gets like that when she has a new boyfriend. She goes all daydreamy and forgetful, and nothing else matters." I feel even more miserable. Thanks, Flora, for picking this Julian guy over me. Thanks a lot.

"I'm sorry, Mollie," Nan says. "I don't know what to say."

"It's not your fault."

"Your mum's doing her best. Try not to be too angry with her. You should talk to her about how you feel. It's important. Don't let it all build up inside. Flora will be sleeping now, so why don't you go down and give Alanna a hand? It might lift your spirits a bit. Sunny will be there. You can try calling Flora later."

"OK. And thanks for telling me the truth, Nan."

I march down the lane towards the cafe, my mind full of Flora and Paris. Maybe Julian's the reason I'm not going with her – maybe the whole insurance thing was just an excuse. I know

Nan said I should talk to Flora, but honestly, trying to talk to my mum about serious stuff is like attempting to film a butterfly or a puppy that won't stay still. She just changes the subject or laughs and tells me to "lighten up". She's impossible!

As soon as I walk through the door of the Songbird Cafe, I get a blast of the smell of baking and hot chocolate, which instantly lifts my mood.

"Boy, am I glad to see you, Mollie!" Alanna appears from the kitchen and wipes her hands on her apron. Her cheeks are bright pink – the kitchen must be hot. "Tell me you've come to help. It's nearly Valentine's Day and I'm so behind with my love potions I could scream."

I expect her to grin. But her face stays serious.

"Love potions, really?" I ask. "Do they work?"

She shrugs. "It's like the remedies – if you believe they work then maybe they do. I've been trying to bring in a bit of extra money by selling them on the Internet. So are you ready to dabble in some spell-making?"

"OK." I can't muster up much enthusiasm. Thoughts of Flora are beginning to fill my head again.

Alanna looks at me for a long second, the gold flecks in her eyes shining. "Nothing bad ever happens in the Songbird. You'll feel all your troubles melt away. I guarantee it. And now, to work, my little love elf."

Sunny is sifting flour into a food mixer in the kitchen. There's a smudge of flour on her cheek.

"Hi, Sunny," I say.

She smiles at me and waves.

"Sunny's on biscuit duty this morning," Alanna says. She hands me a pale blue apron from the back of the door. I take off my hoodie and put the apron on, already feeling more professional.

"Let's get cracking," Alanna says. "First of all, you can stir that. Slowly and carefully." She points to a small copper saucepan that's simmering gently on the hob. I take the wooden spoon and start stirring. Delicious tangy orange smells waft up from the golden-coloured liquid. Alanna starts chopping some dark green leaves, the large knife flying up and down in her hand. She looks like a *MasterChef* winner.

"In the olden days, the love potions were pretty disgusting," she says, adding two pinches of the chopped leaves to my saucepan. "Next the chickweed." She starts chopping up some small white flowers. "They even added things like mice and frogs."

"Like a spell from a fairy tale or the witches in *Macbeth*?" I ask. I put on a spooky voice. "'Double, double toil and trouble; Fire burn and cauldron bubble... Eye of newt and toe of frog, Wool of bat and tongue of dog.'"

Alanna laughs. "Exactly! That's brilliant, Mollie. Clever you. It's Shakespeare, right?"

I nod, chuffed that I remembered it. "Yes. We did it in school."

"Some love potions really were gruesome," Alanna explains. "Like putting a pin into a dead mouse and leaving it to get rusty. If you put the pin in a girl's clothes, she'd follow you all over the world, apparently."

"Yuck!"

"There were worse. Like making tea from boiled gander poo or making the person you fancy eat minced cat liver. Then they'd fall wildly in love with you."

I make a gagging noise, then ask, a little worried, "So what's in this one?"

"Nothing gross, I promise. It's far more romantic: orange blossom and apple. Plus a drop of mistletoe resin, a teaspoon of ground wedding cake and the nectar from a honeysuckle flower that I collected last summer. It's for a woman in Kerry who would like her boyfriend to propose to her. She has to slip three drops of it into his morning coffee every day for a week."

"Why doesn't she ask him herself if she wants to get married so badly?" I ask.

Alanna laughs. "That's a good question. But she wouldn't pay me good money to concoct a potion for her then, would she? Careful now – don't let it boil over." She peers into the saucepan. "OK, I think that's ready. Now we let it cool before bottling it."

"What's next on the job list?" I ask.

"Bunting. Hope you're good with scissors."

We decide on a yellow-and-pale-blue colour scheme for Pancake Day, which is on Tuesday, and red and pink for Valentine's Day on Thursday. We'll put up the heart-shaped bunting on Tuesday evening, after Alanna has served the last pancake. Once she's shown me what to do, Alanna goes back into the kitchen to blend the soup. Sunny and I sit on the sofa in the window, cutting out blue and yellow triangles from thin card and stapling them carefully to blue ribbon. It was a bit fiddly at first, but I'm starting to get the hang of it.

The bell above the door jangles. Lauren strides in, followed by Chloe. Lauren catches sight of me and her cheeks flare. They order two skinny cappuccinos with marshmallows and then retreat into the conservatory.

As they walk past us, the air seems to chill. Or maybe that's just my blood. Sunny puts her hand over mine, her palm warm and solid against my skin.

I ignore the girls' stares and whispers and concentrate on the bunting. I'm trying to act all cool and together, but my body is betraying me. My palms are sticky and my heart is thumping in my chest. I will Lauren to leave me alone. If Landy was here, or even Bonny, I wouldn't feel quite so nervous. I wish this island wasn't so small and there was another cafe to escape to. Then I feel awful – I wouldn't want to go to any cafe that wasn't the Songbird.

"Wish I could cut out paper triangles." Lauren's voice is extra loud. "Wouldn't that be super fun? If I was in preschool."

She and Chloe both giggle.

Keep cutting and stapling, I tell myself. *Don't listen.*

"Shame this place will be closing soon," Lauren continues. "Dad says there's a developer interested in buying the cafe.

Wants to knock it down and build a hotel here instead."

Sunny drops her scissors and they clatter onto the floor.

"Poor Sunny," Lauren says. She and Chloe are standing at the edge of the little conservatory now. "You won't have anywhere to spy on people, will you? A hotel won't let you hang around like a weirdo, scaring off the guests."

"You want to watch yourself, Lauren Cotter," I say.

She puts a hand on her hip, her eyes flashing. "Or what? You'll push me again?"

"I didn't push you and you know it," I say, trying to keep my voice calm. "No, I'll put something in your coffee. Alanna's teaching me all about making potions. I could give you acne or warts."

"Yeah, right," she says, but she looks a bit uncertain. "Anyway, Alanna makes the coffee in here, not you."

"Actually, Mollie's working here now, Lauren." Alanna appears from the kitchen, carrying a tray. "And Landy's just texted to say he's on his way over with a ladder to help the girls put up the bunting. Would you two like to give us a hand as well?"

Lauren blinks rapidly and plays with a strand of her hair. I think the mention of her brother has made her nervous. "Sorry, we're busy," she says. "Can we have those coffees to go, Alanna?"

"Funny you should say that." Alanna nods down at the two white-and-blue Songbird takeaway cups sitting on the tray.

"Did you ask for takeaways?" Lauren asks Chloe.

Chloe shakes her head. "No."

Alanna smiles at Lauren. "Lucky guess."

"Are you trying to tell us we're not welcome here?" Lauren says.

"Not at all," Alanna says. "Everyone's welcome, Lauren. You know that. You should think about being more welcoming yourself. A little birdie told me you've been giving Mollie a hard time. Push her again and you'll have me to deal with. Got it?"

Lauren goes bright red and glares at me. "What have you been saying?" Without waiting for an answer, she slaps a five-euro note down on the nearest table. "Keep the change. I know you need it. What with the cafe closing and everything."

"That's it! Scat, before I lose my temper," Alanna says.

As soon as they've gone, Alanna sits down beside us. She picks up a pair of scissors and starts cutting up the blue and yellow card rather violently.

After a few seconds she says, "For the record, I do have a good acne potion if you ever need it."

"Thanks for sticking up for me then," I say.

"Always, sparrow," she replies, nudging me with her shoulder.

"Sparrow?" I ask.

She smiles. "Yes. You're smart and loyal, just like a sparrow. Sunny's my little nightingale. Together, you're my Songbird Girls. And we Songbirds stick together."

Sunny looks at me and nods firmly.

Landy arrives as we're adding the final touches to the bunting. There's a fold-up metal ladder under his arm. "Lauren isn't still here, is she?" he asks, looking around.

"She just left," Alanna says.

"Phew. So where do you want this bunting?"

With Landy and Sunny's help, it doesn't take long to put up the bunting. There are now jaunty blue and yellow arcs criss-crossing the cafe's ceiling and hanging in the windows. It looks brilliantly festive. Sunny goes home for lunch, but Landy stays. He puts the ladder outside, comes back in and flops down beside me on the sofa.

"It looks grand from out there," he says. "Everyone will be able to see it from the ferry. Nice work, Mollie. Hey, Lauren didn't give you a hard time earlier, did she? Dad told her to keep away from you, but she never listens to anyone, especially not him."

"It was fine." I try to sound convincing. "But I wish she wouldn't tease Sunny about, well, you know."

Landy frowns. "Not speaking, you mean?"

"Yes. I can deal with Lauren's snide comments, but Sunny can't."

"What was she saying exactly?"

"That Sunny was a weirdo who spied on people. She also said something about the cafe closing. And some developers building a hotel. Is that really going to happen?"

Landy exhales slowly, making his fringe lift a little. "Sounds like it. Dad was talking about that at dinner last night. If Alanna can't pay the bank back, she'll have to sell. And the developers are offering a good price."

"Can't Alanna's parents help?"

Landy lowers his voice. "Did Nan not tell you about Alanna's mum and dad?"

Suddenly I realize what I've been missing all along. "They're dead, aren't they?"

He nods silently.

"What happened?" I feel hollow and sad. Poor Alanna.

"Car crash on the mainland. It was icy and they skidded off the road. Alanna lived with her aunt for a while, but that didn't work out so she moved back here and opened her mum and dad's cafe up again. Dad said Alanna had to take out a loan to do the cafe up a bit and build the conservatory."

"This place must be pretty special to her," I say. "Where would she live if it closed down? And what about Sunny and everyone else who needs the cafe?"

Landy gives a deep sigh. "I hear you. But some people think a hotel would be good for the island – bring in more tourists, new jobs. And the bank won't give Alanna any more time to pay back the money she owes. They're putting pressure on her to sell."

I almost jump out of my seat. "That's so wrong! This cafe is special. We have to do something. We have to fight back – let the bank know that they're being unfair, that they should give Alanna a break. If people know the cafe is in danger of closing, they'll visit, and Alanna will be able to pay back the loan. We have to get the news out. Hey, I've got an idea! We should have a protest march."

He laughs. "A march? To where exactly? Up the hill and back down again? Like the Grand Old Duke of York?"

He's teasing me, but I let him get away with it. "OK, maybe not a march. A Save the Songbird Cafe campaign. We can start with an online petition to send to the bank. And I'll ask Sunny to design a campaign poster we can put in the cafe's window and on the ferry. I can make a short film about the Songbird, talk to people who use it, and we can set up our own Facebook page and post the interviews. Once we've raised awareness, we can ask people to send donations to help keep it open."

Landy has that amused smile lingering on his lips.

"What?" I demand. Is he making fun of me again?

"It's a grand idea, Mollser. A brilliant idea, in fact. I can help you with the film if you like, and set up an online petition. When do we start?"

Lunchtime is really busy and Alanna asks me to take the orders – me! I write down what people want in a little notebook, like a proper waitress. Alanna even ropes in Landy to help in the kitchen. He was a bit reluctant at first – "I burn toast, Alanna," he said – but she managed to convince him. I want to say something to Alanna about her parents, tell her how sorry I am, but I know now isn't the right time.

The cafe is mostly full of tourists straight off the one o'clock ferry: birdwatchers dressed in dark green with binoculars around their necks, mums and dads with young kids who all keep asking me, "Where's Click?"

One particular little boy of about six, with a round, freckled face, is driving his grandparents mad with his Click questions. He doesn't seem to like sitting still. He's hopping around like a piece of popcorn in the microwave.

"Hello again, Teddy," Alanna says, passing by his table with a tray. "Click will be here very soon. You keep watching out of the window. I bet if you draw a dolphin picture he'll come even sooner. Mollie will get you some pencils and paper. And if it's really good, I'll give you a lollipop."

"I like lollipops," he says.

As I get the coloured pencils, I spot Alanna slipping out of the door of the cafe. Where's she going when the cafe is so busy? I watch her stand at the harbour wall and raise her hands to her mouth, like she did the first day I was on Little Bird.

Seconds later, Teddy is squealing and pointing out of the window. "Click! I can see him."

Click starts playing in a small fishing boat's wake, leaping into the air and diving back down with a splash.

"I love Click," Teddy says, beaming at me as I give him the pencils and paper. "This is such a cool island. And this is the best cafe ever."

I feel a little sad inside. If the cafe shuts, so many people will lose out. Forcing myself to be brave (I'm not usually all that good at talking to strangers, especially adults), I explain to his granny and grandpa that the cafe may have to close down. I ask them to sign our petition for the bank when Landy has set it up and to make a donation if they can. They think it's terrible that the cafe is in danger and promise to help. Then they thrust ten euros into my hand. Our Save the Songbird Cafe campaign has begun!

As I walk back to Nan's house later that afternoon, my feet are throbbing from standing all day. Now that I'm on my own I start thinking about Flora again and how much she hurts me sometimes. I don't think she means to, but that's just it – she doesn't seem to consider me and my feelings at all. I'm upset about the cafe, too. Poor Alanna. It's so unfair. She works really hard, and it's such an amazing place. Why is everything so rotten sometimes? I put the money the couple gave me in a cookie jar on a shelf in Alanna's kitchen, but a lone ten euros isn't going to go very far.

It's cold, and I shiver and thrust my hands into the pockets of my hoodie. My fingers hit something smooth and cold.

I pull out a small blue bottle – one of Alanna's remedies. She must have slipped it in there earlier. The liquid inside smells like the island – the tang of the sea, mixed with wildflowers and something I can't quite identify, something sweet. I breathe it in and immediately feel less anxious and more determined. I can't get discouraged. I need to start working on the Songbird campaign right now. They can't destroy the cafe – I won't let them. I know Nan will help. I start to run.

Chapter 13

I burst through the door of Summer Cottage like a whirlwind and race down the hallway to the kitchen.

"Nan! Where are you, Nan? I need to use your camera again."

"Goodness, child, you nearly gave me a heart attack," Nan says, clutching her chest. She was making a cup of tea, but she puts the kettle down. Then she reaches for a small brown plastic bottle and pops a pill in her mouth. She washes it down with some water.

"Are you OK?" I ask.

"Just my angina. These are beta blockers. It's nothing to worry about, pet. I think I overdid it in the garden. Weeding is hard work. So what's all this about?"

"Developers are trying to buy the cafe and turn it into a hotel," I say in a rush.

"I know, child. I didn't want to say anything as I knew it would upset you. Awful, isn't it? Having to sell the place is one thing, but seeing it destroyed." She shakes her head. "Poor Alanna."

"That's why we're going to start a campaign to let people know and hopefully raise some money to save it. Landy's going to help and I'll ask Sunny too. I'm going to make a film about the cafe and what it means to people, and put it up on a special Songbird Facebook page. That's why I need your camera."

Nan leans back against the kitchen counter and takes another sip of water. "It's a wonderful idea, Mollie. There's been a building where the cafe is for hundreds of years. It used to be a blacksmith's, way back. They think there was a link with Red Moll's castle. If only we could find proof that Red Moll actually lived on the island, those developers would have a fight on their hands. I can't believe they're thinking of plonking a hulking great hotel right in front of that beautiful castle. It's despicable."

"I thought it was certain she lived there. There must be some record."

"I wish there was. Ellen did a big history project on Red Moll when she was in secondary school. She did a huge amount of research and I helped her. We even went to the National Library, but we couldn't find mention of Little Bird and Red Moll. In fact, there are very few references to Red Moll at all in the documents from that time. Women's lives weren't seen as important in those days."

"But that's so wrong!"

"I know. Ellen felt very strongly about that too. The only place Red Moll's name is mentioned is in the records of her plundering English ships for their cargo and seeing off English generals who tried to take over her family's land, plus some references to her clashes with foreign pirates."

"So are you saying you don't know where Red Moll really lived? What about all those stories Granny Ellen used to tell me? About all the sea battles and scaring off the slave traders? Are you saying they're not true?"

"They're true, all right," Nan says. "And Red Moll did live here – I'm sure of it. Those stories were passed down through generations of McCarthys and O'Sullivans and Cotters and all the other families that have lived on this island for hundreds of years. But unless there's some sort of written document from that time, there's no historical proof."

"Then we have to find proof. There must be something in the castle grounds: old coins, swords – I don't know – bones?" I clench my fists so tightly that my knuckles go white.

Nan shakes her head. "Archaeologists have been combing the castle and the land around it for years and they've never found anything of note. I know it's frustrating, but I think you should focus on the other parts of your campaign." She pauses and smiles sadly. "Ellen would be so proud of you. When she wasn't much older than you are now she organized a protest against the closure of the island's primary school. All the papers covered it and it was even on the six o'clock news. She saved the school." Nan's eyes well up. "Sorry. Let me get a tissue."

As Nan wipes her eyes, I think about Granny Ellen. She told me a lot of stories, about her life as a travel agent and all the different countries she had visited but very few about the island, and none about Nan or PJ. She certainly never mentioned any campaigning – I would have remembered that. I'm discovering a side of her life I never knew, and it makes me miss her more than ever.

After dinner, I'm still fired up about the cafe. I want to do something – now! I've set up the Facebook page and I've posted lots of photos of the island and the cafe. The more I think about it, the stronger I feel about everything. I have to help Alanna. My film about the island needs to be really great. Talking to Nan has given me an idea. I need to include the castle in my film, so people will see how wrong it would be to build a hotel right in front of it, even if I can't prove that Red Moll actually lived there. I should shoot some footage now, at twilight – the ruin will look spectacular against a darkening sky.

Nan is reluctant at first to let me go outside. "Can't you go in the morning? It's brass monkeys out there, child."

"Please?" I beg. "It'll be all dramatic and atmospheric – perfect for our campaign."

"Go on then. If you must. But don't be more than an hour, mind. And you're not stepping outside this house without a coat and welly boots."

Nan gives me a torch and makes me wrap up warmly, winding a woolly scarf around my neck so many times that I almost can't breathe. I take it off as soon as I'm on the lane and stuff it into the pocket of my jacket. I know Nan means well, but what is it with adults and dressing us up like Egyptian mummies? Granny Ellen was just the same.

I'd forgotten how spooky the lane is in the half-light. I can hear rustling in the hedgerows again. I know it's probably just a field mouse, but it still gives me a fright. I whisper, "Lions and tigers and bears, oh my!" to myself as I march along, pretending I'm Dorothy, lost in the woods, in *The Wizard of Oz*. I'm relieved when I get to the road.

I walk towards the harbour, climb over the gate that leads to the castle and tramp across the field in Nan's green welly boots, stomping in a couple of muddy puddles on the way. I'd be too embarrassed to wear wellies in Dublin, but on Little Bird everyone wears them. I hate to admit it, but they're ace for splashing about in and having dry feet is actually pretty cool.

After climbing over the small wall into the field just behind Alanna's cafe, I walk past the mossy old trees, and there it is – the tumbledown remains of Red Moll's castle. Last time I was here I was too angry to think straight. Now, I stand and gaze up at the castle, imagining what it must have been like in Red Moll's day. I spot the ruins of a spiral staircase sticking out from one of the walls, almost hidden by ferns. There must have been a brilliant view of Dolphin Bay from the top of the castle. Maybe that's where Red Moll had her quarters. Granny Ellen told me that Red Moll slept in a four-poster bed and the hawser, or front rope, of her favourite galley ship was attached to one of her bedposts at night. The thought of the boat tied to her bed, like a pet, always makes me smile.

I start to feel a prickling at the back of my neck. I sense I'm not alone. There's someone watching me. Adrenaline washes through my system, making my skin tingle.

I swing around and look at the trees behind me. There's a figure in a red hooded cloak standing at the far side of the field, staring straight at me. I gasp and drop the camera.

"Mollie, it's me – Alanna." She flicks down the hood and walks towards me. "Sorry, I didn't mean to scare you."

My skin is still tingling and my breath quick. "I thought you were Red Moll's ghost!" I pick up Nan's camera and check it over. Luckily it doesn't seem to be damaged.

"I come up here all the time to pick wild plants, and I've never seen her. Although I'd like to – she was an amazing woman. You and Nan are related to her, aren't you?"

"That's right," I say proudly.

"What are you doing up here on your own? And what's with the camera?"

"I'm filming the castle. I hope you don't mind, but we're starting up a Save the Songbird Cafe campaign – me, Landy and Sunny." Nan had Sunny's mum's email address, so I was able to ask her about designing a poster. She got straight back to me and promised to help.

I tell Alanna about all our ideas and about the ten euros I've already hidden in the cookie jar. When I've finished, she says,

"Mind? I'm touched. I don't know what to say. Thank you. I must put all the campaign details up on the cafe's website."

"Good idea. I know I'm new to the island, but you've been really nice to me and I wanted to do something to help. The cafe can't close, Alanna. It just can't."

"So the island is starting to work its charm on you, is it, sparrow?"

"The cafe is. It's a really special place."

"I think so too."

"Alanna…" I hesitate. Now that we're on our own, I want to say something about her mum and dad, but I don't know how to bring it up.

"You know, don't you?" she says quietly. "About my parents."

"Yes. And I'm so sorry."

"Me too," she says. "But don't feel bad for me, Mollie. I love this island and I have good friends here, people who look out for me. I'm very lucky. Now, you should get back to your filming before the light completely fades."

I have a thought. "Alanna, I know this might sound a bit weird, but could you waft around over by the castle and pretend to be Red Moll?"

Alanna laughs. "No problem, Miss Director. I'd be honoured to. Am I pining for my young husband who's away at sea?" She puts on a super-sad face and touches the back of her hand to her forehead. "Or am I fighting off foreign pirates who are trying to invade my castle?" She snarls fiercely and pretends to stab someone with a sword. She looks magnificent, although I don't think the real Red Moll would have worn a green jumper dress with a cat on it under her cloak.

"You're definitely fighting pirates." I put the camera to my eye. "And – action!"

Chapter 14

Tuesday is Pancake Day and I spend most of the afternoon at the cafe. It turns out I'm rather good at making pancakes. Sunny helps too, but she's not great at flipping – most of her attempts end up across the cooker or on the floor – so Alanna puts her in charge of mixing the batter instead. She's better at that. Sunny is seriously smart. She's able to double or treble the batter quantities in her head, no problem.

When I get home that evening, I stink of cooking oil and I have to wash my hair twice to get rid of the smell, but it was a fun day, so I don't mind. We laughed a lot – even Sunny, although her chuckles were mouse-quiet, breathy ones.

On Thursday morning – Valentine's Day – I get a surprise when I walk into the kitchen. Nan has decorated the breakfast table with confetti – tiny red sparkling hearts. There's a napkin with a funny bulge in it beside my plate. Underneath is a cupcake with a large pink heart iced on top. There's also a big red envelope sitting on my cereal bowl. I open it. On the front of the card inside is a cute illustration of a kitten holding a heart. The card reads:

To Mollie,
You are in my heart, always.
All my love,
Nan XXX

Hey, I got a Valentine's card! Although I'm not sure it counts if it's from your great-gran.

Nan walks in then. "Morning, Mollie. Happy Valentine's Day, pet. I'm surprised to see you up at this hour – usually I have to drag you out of bed."

"Thought I'd get to the cafe early," I say. "To help Alanna put up the last of the Valentine's Day decorations."

"That's kind of you." She pauses, her expression going all serious.

Uh-oh, what have I done now?

"I know you like working with Alanna, but you must do the schoolwork your teachers have been setting."

"I did loads yesterday and I'll do some more later." Although I'm not sure when I'll have the time. I need to start editing the footage I've taken of the island and interviewing some of the islanders. Our campaign is going really well so far. Landy's already set up our online petition and Sunny's uploaded the campaign logo she designed to the Facebook page. She drew the words "Save the Songbird Cafe" in beautiful sweeping calligraphy and surrounded the lettering with a border made out of tiny birds, dolphins and butterflies. She's also created a poster for the cafe using the same lettering and motifs.

"Good," Nan says. "I'm glad you're keeping up with your work. And I thought you might like to ring your mum, give her your love and wish her good luck with her news broadcast tonight. Valentine's Day is a time to celebrate everyone we love, including our mums and our great-granddaughters. And I do love you, Mollie. Very much."

I don't know what to say to that. It's nice, but a bit cringey.

She hands me the house phone. "I'll leave you to it. I've put Flora's number in with the right codes. You just need to press the green button. Will you send her my love? Tell her I'll talk to her again soon."

I nod. As soon as Nan has gone, I put the phone down on the kitchen table and sit back in my chair. I still haven't replied to Flora's email. I've been trying to forget about the whole new-boyfriend thing. Do I really want to talk to her? After all, shouldn't *she* be ringing *me*? She's the one who left me on this island so she could go off and see the world.

But I know that being a proper presenter means everything to her and she's probably really nervous about tonight – her first time on the news. Nan's right: I should wish her luck. I pick up the phone and press the green button. The ring tone sounds funny – foreign, I guess.

"Hello?" Flora says cautiously.

"Flora, it's me – Mollie."

"Hi, darling. What a lovely surprise. I thought it was Nan. Hang on a second." I can hear a mumbled conversation in the background before she comes back on the line. "Sorry about that. I'm having coffee with the crew. We're just planning today's filming. Paris is so amazing. The buildings are out of this world." She gives a dreamy sigh. "Every street is like a movie set. We're on our way to the Notre-Dame lock bridge in a few minutes. Pont de l'Archevêché. Phew – nailed it! I've been practising how to pronounce the name all morning. Don't forget to watch me. *Six One News*, yes?"

"Don't worry, I haven't forgotten."

"Oh, and happy Valentine's Day, darling," she gushes. "Did you get any cards?"

"Just one from Nan."

"Sorry I didn't get a chance to send you one. Hang on a second." When she comes back on the line, her voice is flatter. "I'm exhausted, to be honest, Mollie Mops. Utterly worn out. Can't wait to have a good old flop in my hotel later."

"You can always have a rest in the posh hotel in Dublin," I say. "The Merrion, isn't it? I looked at the website. It has a spa and everything. Or will you be too busy with your new boyfriend?"

Flora goes silent. Then she says, "Nan! I'll kill her. I wanted to tell you about Julian myself. It's early days, you see. But I'm glad you know now. And guess what he gave me for Valentine's Day? A whopping big bottle of Chanel No. 5. I got quite a shock. It's very expensive."

"He must really like you."

She giggles. "I think he does. Hang on…" There's a noise in the background and more mumbled conversation. "Sorry, darling, our taxi's just arrived. I'll have to run in a second. Tell me quickly what you've been up to."

"I've been trying to save the Songbird Cafe. Developers want to knock it down and build a hotel instead so we're organizing a campaign." I tell her the plan.

"Lovely," she says, a little absently – she's clearly not listening to me. "That reminds me. Lucas, that's the cameraman, do you know what he's done, the darling boy? He's only gone and put together a whole load of clips of me from the dailies – and set them to music. Little bits of film of me smiling and laughing and making all sorts of funny mistakes. It's adorable. Must have taken him ages."

"When did he give it to you?"

"He emailed the file to me first thing this morning."

"For Valentine's Day?"

She giggles again. "Oh, no, darling." She pauses for a moment. "The email was a bit flowery. He included a poem about treading on dreams or something."

"'Tread softly because you tread on my dreams,'" I say. "It's Yeats. We did it at school."

"Yes! That's it. Aren't you the brainbox, Mollie Mops?"

"Flora! It's definitely for Valentine's Day. He obviously likes you too. What's Julian going to say?"

"I'm hardly going to tell him. Anyway, must run. Big day

today. Kiss, kiss. *Adiós*. Isn't that what they say in France?"

"*Au revoir,*" I say. "And, Flora, you know your Dublin trip? Do you think there's any way—?"

But she's already gone.

I put the phone down, feeling low. Flora didn't say a word about coming to see me on Little Bird, and she rang off before I got the chance to ask her about it. When she's in love, it's as if I don't exist.

At six o'clock, Nan switches on the news and we wait for Flora's piece. It seems to take for ever to come on. There's world news about strikes and uprisings, then national news about milk quotas (whatever they are) and upcoming elections. After an ad break there's the local news and then finally – Flora! She's standing in front of Notre-Dame Cathedral. I recognize it from the guidebook I was reading in the library at school. Its pale stone walls and flying buttresses are lit up with pink and blue lights and it looks spectacular.

Flora's wearing a white coat I don't recognize and a matching white beret. She looks amazing. Seeing her in the flesh makes me realize how much I miss her. She's right there, so close I could reach out and touch her. But if I did, all I'd feel is the smooth screen of Nan's big telly.

Flora walks towards one of the lock bridges. Its sides are covered with shiny metal padlocks. "This is Flora Cinnamon, reporting live from the Pont de l'Archevêché beside Notre-Dame Cathedral in Paris, where sweethearts are celebrating their love this Valentine's Day." She says all this to camera while walking across the bridge. That must be hard, but it doesn't seem to bother her. She seems really comfortable and not at all nervous. I look at her hands – no, not shaking a bit. Halfway across, she stops beside a man and a woman. "Miriam, you are from Slovakia and, Pat, you're Irish. Tell us what you're doing in Paris today."

"Celebrating our five-year wedding anniversary," the pretty blonde woman says. She looks up at her husband. "Pat engraved our initials on the lock himself." She holds up a shiny brass padlock.

"So you're a bit of an old romantic, Pat?" Flora asks him.

"Miriam brings it out in me," he says with a grin. "She's the best." He kisses his wife on the cheek and she beams.

Flora turns back to the camera. "Couples travel here from all over the world to attach a specially engraved lock to the bridge. Miriam and Pat, would you like to do the honours?"

They clip their lock to the thick tapestry of love locks already on the railings while Flora looks on. The locks must make the bridge weigh a ton! She turns to the camera again. "This is Flora Cinnamon, sending you all Valentine's greetings from Paris. *Buonanotte.*" She presses her earpiece against her ear and giggles. "Sorry, I meant *bonne nuit.*"

As soon as the news switches back to the RTÉ studio, Nan turns off the telly and says, "Wasn't she great? You must be so proud of her."

"She was brilliant," I say. "And she didn't seem nervous at all. Apart from the bit at the end when she said good night in Italian instead of French." I imagine Lauren and Chloe laughing at Flora's mistake and my stomach clenches.

Nan smiles. "But she made a great recovery. Your mum's a natural on camera. And this travel show's going to make her a household name."

"She's going to be famous, you mean?" I hadn't really thought of that.

"Yes, I expect so. In Ireland, anyway."

Great – she'll be busier than ever. Just what I need! I know I should be pleased for Flora, but it's hard. I wish she'd make time for me and listen to me for a change. I wish I could talk to her about how I feel. How can I make her understand how much I need her? She may not be perfect, but she's the only mum I have.

"How did your phone call go earlier?" Nan asks, as if she can tell something's wrong.

"OK. We didn't get much time to talk."

"You miss her a lot, don't you?"

I nod, not trusting myself to talk without my voice cracking.

"Go and email her, pet. Tell her all the things you wanted to say, but didn't get the chance to. Tell her how much you miss her. She might change her mind about coming to Little Bird if she realizes how much you'd love to see her. It's worth a try."

* * *

Sent: Thursday 14 February 18:30
From: molliemops@irelandmail.ie
To: floracinnamon21@gmail.ie
Subject: You were amazing on the news

Hello Big TV Star,

You were awesome! I would have gone all tongue-tied and fallen into the Seine or something. You rocked it, Flora! Nan says you're a natural and that you're going to be famous soon. I think she's right.

There's something I didn't get to say to you on the phone earlier. I miss you so much. I know it's a big ask, but can't you come to Little Bird to see me when you're back in Dublin? Nan might be able to bring me to the mainland, if that suits you better. I could even get the bus up to Dublin for the day. Please, Flora? I really want to see you. I feel like you're off travelling and doing all these cool things and you've kind of forgotten about me. I know it's silly, but I can't help how I feel. Please can I see you? PLEASE!

Love you,

Mollie XXX

Chapter 15

When I wake up the following morning, the curtain is slightly open and a ray of sunlight is shining on the painting of Red Moll. Still half asleep, I think it's Granny Ellen in the picture for a second. Then I lie in bed for a while, thinking about Granny Ellen and then about Flora. I wonder if she has read my email yet. I get up to see.

Nan's laptop is on my desk so I log into my email. Yes! A reply. That was quick. I click on it, feeling excited.

Sent: 15 February 1:05
From: floracinnamon21@gmail.ie
To: molliemops@irelandmail.ie
Subject: A quick note from a tired presenter...

Hi Mollie Mops,
Thank you, darling. I was so happy it went well. Even Julian said it was good and it takes a lot to impress him. He teased me about the "buonanotte" thing, said it was a silly mistake and I guess he's right. But Lucas told

me not to mind Julian one bit. He said viewers aren't bothered by slip-ups. They like presenters they can relate to, like me. He's a real doll, Lucas.

Now about coming to visit... I'm so sorry, Mopsy. I did talk to Julian about squeezing in a trip to Little Bird, but it just isn't possible. I really, really want to see you, but it's all too tight. Julian has our time carefully mapped out. He's very organized that way. We only have one day to ourselves and then it's back to the studio for editing.

I'll ring you when I'm in Dublin, though, promise, and we'll have a nice long chat. And I'll be back in no time. The next few weeks will fly by. You'll see.

Is everything OK with Nan? I hope this isn't all too much for her. I know she was worried about having you – in fact, I had to practically beg her to take you in. You are being good, aren't you?

I'll buy you something cool in Rome. What do you fancy? And if I buy myself the lush Prada sunglasses I've been swooning over, you can have my old Gucci pair with the cute gold arms. What do you think? I know you love them.

Better run! Filming up the Eiffel Tower today.

Love, love, love,

Flora XXX

P. S. Miss you too, darling!

* * *

"Morning, Mollie." Nan is standing in her favourite place – with her back to the Aga, warming her bum – when I walk into the kitchen.

"Morning." The table is all set for breakfast, with delicious-looking breakfast muffins, but even that doesn't lift my mood.

"What has your mum said now?" Nan asks.

"What do you mean?"

"The long face. I'm guessing it has something to do with Flora. She's not coming to see you, is she?"

"I don't want to talk about it."

Nan sighs. "I'm going to have a word with her, pet, remind her of her responsibilities. That girl needs a good shake sometimes."

"Don't bother! You told me to email her, tell her how I felt. Well, I did what you said and it didn't make any difference. All she thinks about is her stupid career and her stupid new boyfriend. She doesn't listen to a word anyone else says."

"I know it must seem that way, but it's not true. Come here to me." She reaches out to give me a hug, but I dodge her arms.

"You're just as bad. Flora told me the truth about having to beg you to let me stay. I know you don't want me here, so I'll try to keep out of your way. If I had somewhere else to go, I would. But I don't."

"Mollie—" I'm out of the front door before she gets the chance to say anything else.

Nan follows me. "Please don't run off again. Yes, I had reservations about having you to stay. But it's not for the reasons you think. I love having you here."

I pick up speed, but she's not giving up.

"Mollie, please come back!" Nan runs after me. "I need to explain."

"Leave me alone! I hate you all!"

"Mollie!" she calls after me. "Mollie!"

I ignore her and sprint down the lane and onto the road. I don't stop until I'm at the gate that leads to Red Moll's castle.

I check behind me to make sure Nan isn't following. She'll definitely look for me in the cafe, so I climb over the gate and walk towards the castle. I'm completely fed up – with Flora and with Nan. Lauren was right – no one wants me. And it hurts. My eyes sting with tears. It's like when I first arrived all over again. Except it's not, not really.

I stare down at the roof of the Songbird and think about how kind Alanna's been to me. Nan too, if I'm being honest. Even if she didn't want me here in the beginning, she's always made me feel welcome.

I think about my new friends, Sunny and Landy. When I first got to the island, I hated Landy for laughing at me and making me feel like a complete outsider. But things are different now – it's almost like I belong.

I shouldn't have shouted at Nan. I have to go back and talk to her, tell her I'm sorry.

* * *

I get an awful fright when I find Nan halfway down the lane, collapsed on the ground. Her eyes are closed and she's clutching her chest. I've never seen anyone look so grey and sick.

"Nan!" I cry. "Nan!" I crouch down beside her and shake her gently, but there's no response. Has she had a heart attack? Oh no! It's all my fault. If I'd stayed and listened to what she had to say instead of running off, she wouldn't have dashed after me.

My hands shaking, I pull out my mobile and find Landy's number, praying that he picks up. It rings several times. *Answer,* I beg. *Please answer.*

"Hey, Mollie, what's up? You're lucky you caught me. I'm on my way to maths class."

"It's Nan," I say in a rush. "She's unconscious. I don't know what's happened. Help me, please. She won't wake up."

"It's going to be all right, Mollser. Stay with her. I'll ring Dad. He'll know what to do. Where are you?"

After I tell him, he rings off with another, "It'll be OK."

Nan stirs a little and moans.

Tears prick my eyes as I put my arms around Nan. "Please get better," I murmur. "Please, Nan."

Chapter 16

Bat's jeep comes racing up the lane, sending dust and small stones flying. He stops and then jumps out of the driver's seat.

"How's Nan doing, Mollie?" he says, sprinting towards us.

"Not great," I say. "I think she's finding it hard to breathe."

Bat hunkers down and looks at Nan. He strokes her head gently. "Hang in there, Nan. Help's on the way."

Nan's eyelids flutter, but she doesn't open them. At least she seems able to hear him.

"The helicopter will be here in about twenty minutes with paramedics on board," Bat tells me. "There's no hospital on the island. We're lucky – it was already in the air on a training session. Do you have any idea what happened?"

I open my mouth to tell him, but there's a lump in my throat and I can't speak. I swallow. I'll have to talk to the paramedics soon so I may as well get it over with. I take a deep breath.

"We had a fight," I admit. "She was running after me. I got as far as Red Moll's castle, then I turned back. I found her here, on the ground. Is it her heart?"

"From the look of things, I'd say yes. Nan's had heart problems for a while. These things happen, Mollie. Don't blame yourself. What's important now is that we get Nan treated. The helicopter will land in the campsite and I'll bring the paramedics here in the jeep. Then, if they can move her, they'll take Nan to the hospital on the mainland."

"Can I go with her?" I say.

"I don't think they'll let you travel in the helicopter. If that's the case, I'll drive you there myself. Nan has always been very kind to me. And us islanders stick together."

Bat's right about me not being allowed to travel with Nan in the helicopter. The paramedics say they'll be faster without me and that every minute is critical.

The paramedics are kind but businesslike. When I tell them what happened – that Nan was running after me and collapsed – they don't blink. They just ask medical questions. *How long was she lying there for? Is she on any medication?*

"Yes," I tell them, suddenly remembering. "Blockers or something. Does that make sense? For her … her…" I try to think of the word. "Angina."

"Beta blockers," one of them says. "Thanks. That's really helpful."

They carefully put Nan onto a stretcher and then carry her to the helicopter. It takes off, whipping grass clippings and dead leaves into the air. I watch until it's a speck in the sky and I can't hear the whirring of the blades any more.

Then Bat says, "We should ring your mum. Do you have her number?"

Of course! Why didn't I think of that? I pull out my mobile, but then I stop for a second. I'm still angry about Flora's Dublin email. Then I think about how serious this is – Nan is on her way to hospital – and I quickly find her number. It goes straight to messages.

"Flora," I say. "Nan's being airlifted to hospital. It's her heart." Then I pause, the reality of the situation finally sinking in. If Nan's in hospital and I can't get through to Flora, what happens to me? I can't stay in Nan's house on my own. I'm completely alone. And then I feel guilty for thinking about myself when Nan's so sick. "Can you ring me, Flora? As soon as you get this?" I end the call and turn to Bat. "She's not answering."

"I'm sure she'll ring you back soon. Now, the next ferry isn't until five. Would you like to wait at our house?"

I shake my head because I realize I'm not on my own any more. There's somewhere I can always go. "Can you take me to the Songbird Cafe?"

When we arrive, Alanna is standing just inside the doorway, as if she's expecting us. She's twisting one of her apron strings around her hand.

"I heard a helicopter," she says immediately.

I'm so relieved to see her that I start to cry. Alanna gives me a hug. "It's OK, Mollie," she says gently, stroking my head.

"What's happened, Bat? Is it Nan?"

"Yes." He quickly explains what happened, then says, "I'm going to find Mattie to see if the ferry can make a special trip across to the mainland now."

When Bat has gone, I say quietly, "It's my fault that Nan got hurt." And I tell her how I ran off and Nan followed me.

Alanna puts her arm around me again. "Nan has had heart problems for a while. She wasn't sure if she was up to looking after a teenager, in fact. But then you arrived, all grown up, and she stopped worrying. She's tough. She'll pull through – you'll see."

I feel even worse knowing why Nan wasn't sure about having me here. I start crying again.

"Trust me – she'll be fine," Alanna says. "And I'm coming to the hospital with you. My poor little Songbird. Hang in there, sparrow."

It's eight o'clock in the evening and I've been sitting in the waiting area of the Accident and Emergency Department of the hospital for a long time. Nan's in the Resuscitation Unit. Bat's here with me, plus Landy and Alanna. Landy insisted on coming with us. Bat told his school it was a family emergency and collected him on the way here. It's nice to have friends with me. Talking to them makes me less scared and worried about Nan. We're waiting to talk to Dr Riesman, Nan's doctor.

The room smells of disinfectant and the bright fluorescent lights are giving me a headache. Every now and then Alanna reaches over, squeezes my hand and says things like, "No news is good news," and, "We'll hear something soon."

Landy's head is bowed. He's playing a game on his iPhone. Bat's outside taking a phone call. The large clock on the wall goes *tick, tick, tick*. The wait is excruciating. The nurse said that Nan was in the best possible hands, but she couldn't tell us anything more. At least we know she's alive.

Finally one of the doors swings open and a doctor in a white coat walks out, holding a clipboard. She's tall and her light brown hair is in one of those tight buns that look like a doughnut.

"Mollie Cinnamon?" She looks around the waiting room.

"Here," I say, my voice coming out as a squeak.

She nods briskly. "Do you have an adult with you?"

"Yes, me," Alanna says.

It's funny – I never think of Alanna as an adult, but technically I guess she is.

The doctor nods again. "OK, good. I'm Doctor Riesman. I'm looking after Mrs McCarthy." She looks at me. "And you are her grandchild, correct?"

"Great-granddaughter," I say. "I'm staying with her at the moment."

"Mrs McCarthy is stable now," she explains. "She's on a heart monitor and her breathing is regular."

The rush of relief is overwhelming. I feel like I'm about to cry again, so I take a deep breath to calm myself. "She's OK?" I ask. "Really?"

The doctor nods. "She's weak at the moment, but she's going to be fine."

"That's great news," Alanna says.

"Yes, but was it a heart attack?" I ask the doctor.

"There are early indications of that," she says. "Or severe angina. But we won't know until we run some more tests."

"How long will she be in hospital for?" I ask. "Can I see her?"

"It depends on the results. But it may only be a few days. If there's any change in her condition, I'll let you know. For now she has to rest, but you'll be able to visit her later."

"Thank you, Doctor," Alanna says.

Once Dr Riesman has gone, Alanna puts her arm around my shoulder. "I know all this must be hard for you and you're coping brilliantly. But you heard what the doctor said – Nan is stable and she'll be out of here soon. It's fantastic news."

I nod wordlessly, relief overwhelming me. I don't trust myself to speak without bursting into tears.

My mobile rings. I recognize the number and answer it immediately. "Flora! Finally!"

"I'm so sorry, darling," she says. "I was filming. Are you all right? And how's Nan?"

"Hang on a sec," I say. "I don't think you're supposed to be on your mobile in here."

I walk down the corridor and through the main doors into the hospital car park. It's cold outside, but I don't mind. After the muggy heat of the waiting area, it's refreshing.

"I'm at the hospital," I tell her. "The doctor says that Nan's stable now and she's breathing regularly. She thinks it might have been a heart attack, but she has to do more tests."

"Oh my goodness, poor Nan. Darling, I'm on my way to the airport. I'll get there as quickly as I can."

"But you're in Paris. What about work?"

"Work, schmirk. Oh, Mopsy, of course I'm coming. I'll be there soon. I love you, darling."

As I click off the phone, I smile. Flora has finally come through for me.

Chapter 17

Flora arrives at the hospital at seven o'clock the following morning. I hear her before I see her.

"Could you be an absolute angel and tell me where I can find Mrs Nan McCarthy?"

I've been lying across the plastic seats trying to get some sleep, but at the sound of her voice I open my eyes. Alanna's dozing opposite me and Bat and Landy are in the car park, sleeping in the jeep. The night seemed to go on for ever and my neck and back are horribly stiff.

Flora's at the desk talking to one of the receptionists. She's wearing a smart camel-coloured coat with shiny gold buttons, and she has new designer sunglasses perched on top of her head. Even at this hour of the morning she looks amazing. Like a real superstar.

"She was brought in yesterday," Flora continues. "I'm also looking for Mollie Cinnamon, her great-granddaughter. She's only twelve, you see, and I'm most awfully worried about her. I'm her mum."

"Over here, Flora," I say, waving.

She lets out a squeal, rushes over and swamps me in a hug. I smell her familiar sweet perfume and feel so relieved to have her here with me. Then I draw back. I'm glad to see her, of course I am, but during the night I kept remembering that it's taken a heart attack to get her back to me.

"Oh, my poor darling," she says. "Have you been here all night? Alone?"

"Alanna's with me," I say. I point to Alanna, who is still sound asleep, with one of her long plaits dangling over the side of the chair like Rapunzel's hair. "She's my friend from the island. And Landy and Bat are outside. Bat drove us all up here yesterday. He's one of Nan's neighbours."

"And where's Nan?" Flora asks.

"She's still in the Resuscitation Unit. They're trying to find her a bed on a ward. They won't let us see her yet – she's resting."

"But she's all right?"

"Yes. The doctor says she's going to be fine."

"Thank goodness for that." She flops down on the seat beside me. "Oh, Mopsy, I'm so glad to see you, but I am bushwhacked. I didn't get a wink of sleep. All that rushing around airports. I had to fly into London in the end and then on to Dublin. But I guess you had a rotten night too, didn't you, poppet?" She rests her head on my shoulder. "Once we've got the latest from Nan's doctor, and they find her a bed, how about you and me book into the fanciest, schmanciest hotel and get some shut-eye? Let your friends go home. I'll get the hospital to ring us as soon as Nan's well enough for a visit, and we can whizz straight over to see her. Does that sound like a plan?"

I nod. I'm too exhausted to work out how I feel about Flora right now. She has come a long way to be here. And a comfy hotel bed does sound like heaven.

Later that afternoon, after a long nap and a huge feed in a swanky hotel beside the river, we return to the hospital in a taxi. Flora looks amazing. She's wearing a new pair of designer jeans, a seal-grey silk shirt and a long gold necklace with a crystal dangling from it that swings like a pendulum when she moves. Bat left earlier – he's driving Alanna and Landy home. They were all so kind to keep me company. I think when you've been through something really tough and scary like that, it bonds you together in a special way. When I waved them off outside the hospital, I felt sad to be saying goodbye.

The hospital has found Nan a bed in a shared ward. When Flora and I get there, most of the women in the five other beds are sleeping, but not Nan. She's sitting up at the far end of the room, her back resting against a snowdrift of pillows. Her face is a lot pinker now and she looks a hundred times better than yesterday. I feel instantly lighter and less worried.

Flora seems a little hesitant, so I lead the way. "Nan?"

As soon as she sees me, she smiles. "Mollie. Aren't you a sight for sore eyes. And Flora. My goodness, is it really you? And so beautiful. Just like Mollie. The nurses told me you were here earlier, but I didn't quite believe them."

"Can we sit down?" Flora asks.

"Of course." Nan is studying Flora with wonder, as if she's an exotic animal that everyone thought was extinct. Then I remember – Flora was fifteen the last time she visited the island, for PJ's funeral. It must be pretty strange for Nan to see her in person again.

As Flora goes off to find a second chair, Nan says, "I must have given you quite a scare, child. Are you all right?"

I nod and pull my chair in closer to Nan's bed. "I'm so sorry, Nan. I should never have run off or said all those things to you. Alanna said you'd been worried about something like this happening. And it did."

"Hush, child," Nan says. "It's not your fault."

Flora places a chair beside mine. She drapes her coat over the back and then sits down, taking one of the coat's arms and holding it like a comfort blanket. Her hand is shaking a little. It's not like Flora to be so nervous.

"That's a beautiful coat," Nan says.

"Thank you," Flora says. "It's cashmere."

"Ellen loved clothes too. Even as a child. Always such a stylish dresser."

At the mention of Granny Ellen's name, Flora winces. "I don't usually talk about Mum in front of Mollie."

"Mollie loved her granny very much," Nan says. "She should be allowed to talk about her. Ellen would have wanted—"

"How do you know what she would have wanted?" Flora

154

says, a little sharply. "You weren't part of her life once she left the island. You didn't know her the way I did."

Nan sighs. "That wasn't my choice."

"What happened, Nan?" I cut in. Now is probably the wrong time to ask, but if I don't, I may never get another chance. Nan and Flora will just clam up as usual and refuse to tell me anything. "What happened between you and Granny Ellen?" I continue. "I know you had a big fight, but what was it about? Flora won't talk about it and Granny Ellen always changed the subject. I'm tired of all these secrets. Please?"

Nan looks at Flora. Flora gives a tiny nod.

"Ellen left the island when she was eighteen to go to teacher-training college," Nan says, her voice soft. "She told us her plan was to work with PJ eventually in the island school. But she changed her mind. She dropped out of college without discussing it with us first, to work in a travel agent's. It broke your great-grandpa's heart. After that we never really got on. I was furious with her for upsetting PJ and shutting us out like that. She was angry with me for not supporting her choice. We said some things to each other that we shouldn't have. It was stupid. We were too alike in many ways – both headstrong and stubborn. Neither of us would back down. Over the years it got harder and harder to build bridges. Ellen stopped visiting the island and we stopped talking, even over the phone. I never even met her husband, your grandad. The last time I saw her was at PJ's funeral and even then we barely spoke. It's the greatest regret of my life."

Nan coughs a little and pushes herself up in the bed. She turns to Flora. "I never dreamed I'd lose her so early – before I could apologize for all the hurt I'd caused her. Yes, we had our differences, but I loved her more than anything. I hope she knew that." Nan's eyes well up and she blinks back the tears.

"I think in her heart she did," Flora says, her voice gentler now. "Mum just wanted a different kind of life. And she wanted you to be OK with that. She never talked about Little Bird, but I often caught her looking through the old photos she took to Dublin with her. Of you and Grandpa and the island." She pauses. "I'm sorry I asked you not to come to her funeral. That was wrong. I wasn't thinking straight."

Nan puts her hand on Flora's. "That's OK, child. It would have upset me too much anyway. We've all made mistakes. I'm hoping we can put the past behind us and start again. Can we do that, Flora? Make a new start?"

Flora looks at me and then back at Nan. "Yes, I'd like that. I should have brought Mollie to see you a long time ago. It's just been so busy. TV-filming schedules – they are so crazy! You barely get a minute to yourself. It's been wonderful of you to take Mollie. I hope it wasn't too much." Flora looks a little guilty.

"Don't be thinking like that, child," Nan says. "What happened happened, and it's no one's fault. I just have to be a bit more careful, that's all. I need to stop racing around like a teenager, the doctor says." Nan smiles at Flora. "I love having Mollie around to liven things up. Thank you for trusting me with her. We've been having a grand old time, haven't we, Mollie?"

"Yes," I say. "You've been brilliant. Now, can I ask you something else?"

"Of course," she says. "Anything."

"You call *me* child, Nan," I say. "And you call Flora that too. When does it stop? When we're fifty?"

Nan gives a little laugh. "Never. I'll always call you both child. It's what I call the people I love. My family."

I shrug. "I guess in that case I can live with it."

"Me too," Flora says.

Later in our hotel room, I curl up against Flora in the double bed, like I used to do when I was little.

"Night, Mopsy," she whispers to me. "Don't let the bedbugs bite."

"Night, Flora."

That night, I sleep like a baby.

Chapter 18

The following afternoon, after visiting Nan, Flora and I catch the bus to the ferry. Nan insisted we went back to the island. She said she was on the mend and that I was starting to look like a scarecrow in my creased clothes.

Mattie is standing on the harbour wall, collecting fares. "Good to see you, Mollie," she says as soon as she spots me. "How's Nan?"

"Much better," I say. "They have to do something called a stress test today, to see if her heart is all right. The doctor says if everything's good she can go home on Tuesday. They think it was her angina, not a heart attack."

Mattie smiles. "That's brilliant news. And who is this then?" she asks, staring at Flora.

I'm used to the islanders' curiosity by now, so I just say, "Flora, this is Mattie Finn, from the island. And, Mattie, this is my mum, Flora. She's coming to stay on Little Bird for a few days. To look after Nan."

"And you, young lady," Flora says with a grin.

"Flora, of course!" Mattie says. "Haven't seen you for years.

You're the spit of your mum. I was sorry to hear she had passed away."

"Thanks," Flora says, her eyes sad. "We miss her, don't we, poppet?"

"Yes," I say, surprised at her question. It's the first time she's admitted it in front of me. "We miss her a lot."

Flora squeezes my hand.

Flora isn't great on boats, which is kind of ironic given her travel show and everything. She feels seasick in the cabin, so we have to sit up on deck, in the fresh air. We settle ourselves down on the right-hand side of the ferry, out of the wind, and once we're under way Mattie brings us some yellow oilskins.

"Tuck these around your legs," she says. "It'll stop you freezing to death."

When Mattie's gone, Flora snuggles up against me. I can feel her warmth through her cashmere coat.

"Are you OK, Flora?" I ask as we chug out of the harbour towards Little Bird. Her face is going a bit green.

She nods. "I'm OK, Mopsy. And it is rather pretty, if you like all that nature kind of stuff. That's the island over there, isn't it? It's all coming back to me now. The harbour and the pink and yellow houses."

"That's Little Bird, all right." I smile to myself. I thought the pastel-coloured houses were ridiculous at first, but now they're growing on me. It's funny – I never thought in a million years that I'd say it, but I've missed the island and I can't wait to get back.

First thing the next morning we walk down to the cafe for some hot chocolate and cake. Flora stumbles a little on the lane in her platform runners – I'm wearing wellies – but finds it easier when we get to the road. It's a bright, sunny day and she's wearing her new Prada sunglasses. When we got to Nan's house last night, she was surprised by how comfy and warm it was, just as I had been when I arrived. She said it's been renovated since she last stayed there, but she remembers the view from Granny Ellen's room and the garden.

I cooked dinner last night. Nothing fancy – just spaghetti carbonara, which Nan showed me how to make – but Flora was dead impressed. "Look at you, all grown up," she said.

"I'd forgotten how quiet the island is," she says now as we pass the gate that leads to Red Moll's castle.

She's right – it is quiet. The only noise is the sound of songbirds twittering in the hedgerows. There are no traffic sounds, no school children shouting across the road to friends, no old ladies chatting at the bus stop.

"I guess it is," I say.

"And the air's so fresh. Not like Paris. Don't get me wrong – it's an amazing city, but they have a big problem with smog at the moment. Some days you're not even allowed to use a car in the city centre. You have to walk or get public transport."

As soon as she says the word Paris, I feel my back stiffen. I start to walk a little quicker.

"Slow down," Flora says.

I go even faster.

"Woah there, Mopsy!"

I ignore her.

"Mollie! What on earth's wrong?"

I swing around. "If you can't guess, I'm not telling you."

"What are you talking about? Come on, darling, help a girl out. Have I said something wrong?"

I give a dramatic sigh. "It's all about you, isn't it, Flora? Me, me, me. My precious travel show. All the fab places I've been to." I take off her voice. "'OMG, Paris is, like, soooo amazing. And Sydney is soooo amazing. And Julian is soooo amazing. And, like, we're soooo in love I have to spend every minute with him and I can't possibly visit my daughter even though she's only practically down the road.'" By the end I'm almost shouting.

Flora goes pale. She lifts her sunglasses so she can see me clearly. "Oh, Mopsy. I'm sorry. I know how much you wanted to go to Paris. But it wasn't meant to be. We'll go soon, darling – just the two of us. And I do wish you could meet Julian. Then you'd understand why I'm so mad about him and why I was so excited about the hotel trip. He really is dreamy."

I roll my eyes at her. "Flora!"

"Sorry. And, Mopsy, if you wanted to see me so badly why didn't you tell me?"

"I did! In my email, remember? I begged you to come and see me. You didn't pay any attention. You kept going on about sunglasses and the Eiffel Tower. You're so lost in your own world sometimes, you don't think about me."

Flora looks uncomfortable. "I do think about you, Mollie. All the time. I just get a bit carried away. I'll try harder – really I will. And you'll only be here a few more weeks. To be honest, I'm sick of travelling. I thought I'd love all the gadding about, but I'm wrecked. If I have to see the inside of another airport, I'll scream. I just want to be home, with you." She pauses. "You do want to come home, don't you, darling?"

I don't answer. The truth is I want to be with Flora, but I also want to be here. Leaving the island would mean leaving Alanna and Landy and Sunny and the cafe, not to mention Nan. And I wonder how much Flora has really changed.

"I am so sorry about Paris," Flora says. "And I promise on my life that we'll go there together ASAP. Can you forgive me, Mopsy?"

Her eyes are all big and sad, like a puppy's. How can I say no? Flora is just Flora. I don't think she means to be so hopeless. I say I forgive her and she pulls me into an enormous squashy hug.

Alanna is thrilled to see us. "How's my Songbird girl this morning?" she asks. "And, Flora, nice to see you again."

We called in briefly yesterday to fill Alanna in on Nan's progress. I'm not sure Flora knew quite what to make of

Alanna at first. I guess her dress sense can be a little theatrical at times and her sunflower-yellow dungarees were very bright. Today she's in her green jumper dress with the cat on it, with black cat's ears on her headband.

"What can I get you?" Alanna asks. "Let me guess – an Americano and a hot chocolate? And there are some red-velvet cupcakes just out of the oven."

"Perfect," Flora says. "Mollie's been telling me all about your delicious cupcakes. I can't wait to try one."

We sit on the sofa in front of the window. Flora looks around the cafe, taking in the conservatory dancing with sunbeams, the kitchen dresser full of cupcakes on pretty cake stands and the view of the fishing boats bobbing in the harbour.

"I can see why you like this place so much, Mollie Mops. There's something magical about it, isn't there?"

"Yes," I say forcefully. "Which is why we have to save it."

"Save it? What do you mean?"

I knew she hadn't been listening properly when I told her about our campaign on the phone. "Alanna owes the bank money and they're not giving her enough time to pay it back," I explain. "They're trying to make her sell the cafe to these property developers. They want to knock it down and build a hotel. We've started a campaign to save it. See…" I point to one of Sunny's posters, hanging in the window. "But so far we only have eighty-one signatures on our online petition for the bank and only a few people have made donations. I don't know what else to do."

Flora is quiet for a moment. Then she says, "I could ask Julian, Mopsy. He might have some good ideas. And I'll sign your petition if it helps."

"Thanks, Flora." That makes eighty-two signatures. It's nowhere near enough. We need to make a bigger impact or else there won't be a Songbird Cafe and Alanna's heart will break. I can't let that happen. I just can't.

Chapter 19

"Are you sure they're coming, Flora?" I ask for the millionth time. "I don't see a camera crew on the ferry."

"There'll just be the two of them," Flora says. "Lucas and Davida, the news reporter. I wish I could present the piece instead, but as I'm your mum it wouldn't be right."

Here's the funny thing – it was Lucas who came through for Flora in the end, not Julian. Julian said he was far too busy to worry about some cafe on an island in the middle of nowhere. Luckily Lucas said he'd help instead. In fact, he insisted.

Turns out Julian is not so dreamy after all and Flora promptly broke up with him. She says she's more disappointed than sad. She thought Julian was different to all the selfish men she'd gone out with in the past.

"Only two people?" I say now.

Flora laughs. "Try not to look so disappointed, Mopsy. That's all we need – a cameraman and a presenter. Lucas is a director, too. He'll edit the piece and all being well it will be on *Six One News* tonight."

"You mean they might not show it?"

She shrugs. "Something big might come up, like an earthquake or a landslide. I just don't want you to get your hopes up." Flora smoothes down my hair.

I whip my head away. "Hey! Watch the hair."

She laughs. We've been getting on pretty well over the last two days. I think clearing the air by telling her how I felt about everything really helped. Yesterday we talked more about Paris and why I had been so upset. I explained that it wasn't just the cancelled trip that had annoyed me. It was the fact that she hadn't even checked with the production company before promising me I could go. Plus, making poor Nan break the news to me wasn't very kind. I told her I was sick of being disappointed all the time and hearing about it from someone else. She has to start telling me the truth herself, even if it's bad news.

"I'm sorry," she said. "I've never been very good at having difficult conversations. You know that I tend to brush things under the carpet and hope they'll go away. I'll try harder, I promise. I want to be a good mum and be there for you. But it's important that I work, too. I didn't go to college or anything. I just did that media course. I want to make something of myself and I want you to be proud of me. It's really important to me."

"I *am* proud of you, Flora," I said.

"Really? I thought you saw me as a bit of an airhead."

"Flora! You're not an airhead. You're a brilliant presenter and I'm very, very proud of you."

"That means a lot to me, darling. Thank you. And I've been

doing some thinking over the past few days. I've been asked to do a second series of *Travelling Light*. Lucas is taking over from Julian as director, and he promises the filming schedule won't be as hectic this time. But it will mean a lot more foreign trips over the next few months. I can't take you with me, so it would mean staying here with Nan for a while. How would you feel about that?"

I didn't know what to say, so I just shrugged.

"It's your choice, darling. If you want me to leave the programme, I will. I mean it. I want to be the best mum I can be, Mollie. I know I haven't always put you first, but that's going to change. So it's up to you – Little Bird or Dublin? You don't have to tell me right now. Think about it, OK?"

I was thinking about it all night. And it's still on my mind now. I miss Dublin – the shops, the cinema, Shannon – but Little Bird isn't so bad. In fact, I'm starting to quite like living here. And I've made some good friends already. It's a really difficult decision.

"There they are," Flora says, waving at two figures on the ferry. "Let's get this show on the road."

"OK, Mollie," Flora says, all efficient. I've never seen her in work mode and she's a different person – calm and organized. "Davida's going to ask you why you think the cafe should be saved. Talk nice and slow. I know you're nervous, but just tell her why you love the cafe so much and what it means to the island."

I'm standing at the cafe door and my stomach is full of butterflies. I look at the crowd gathered around. So far I've counted sixty-three people in total – quite a turnout for such a small island. Some of Bat's birdwatching friends have come a long way to support the cafe, along with lots of other people from the mainland. The only person who's missing is Nan. Bat's collecting her from the hospital right now. They're due back on the six-thirty ferry.

Alanna is here too, of course, trying to look hopeful rather than sad. Sunny is here with her mum and little sister, and so are Landy, Bonny and, worse luck, Lauren and Chloe. Lauren is standing at the front of the crowd, wearing too much make-up and tossing her hair around like a diva. I think she wants to be on the telly, but Davida hasn't noticed her. Or if she has, she's ignoring her. Davida's already done an interview with Alanna. It was heartbreaking. When Davida asked her what she'd do if the cafe closed, Alanna's eyes filled with tears and she just shook her head. "I have no idea," she said. "It's been in my family for generations. It's my life." She got a huge round of applause from the crowd when she finished.

"That was brilliant," Flora said, hugging her. "Don't give up, Alanna. It's not over yet."

"Pay no attention to the camera," Lucas tells me, as he moves me to stand just under the cafe's sign, ready for my interview. "Just look at Davida and answer her questions. You're probably like me – happier behind a camera."

I nod. "Much happier."

Lucas is tall, with dark brown eyes and cropped black hair and his face is very serious until he smiles. Luckily he smiles a lot, and from the way he gazes at Flora and laughs very loudly at her jokes, he clearly adores her.

I wasn't sure how I felt about this when he first arrived, but I'm getting used to it. And unlike some of Flora's ex-boyfriends, he doesn't talk to me like I'm five years old. Flora told him I've been taking video footage of the island – I showed her some of it last night – and he said he'd love to see it. He even said I can have a go on his camera later – although it looks a bit heavy for me to carry. He's not dreamy or Hollywood handsome, but he is really nice.

Davida stands beside me as Lucas adjusts the camera. "Ready?" she asks him.

"Ready," he says.

Davida shakes out her hair and then smiles at the camera.

"I'm on Little Bird Island with Mollie Cinnamon, a direct descendant of the infamous pirate queen Red Moll. Mollie is one of the people behind the campaign to save the island's only cafe. Mollie, can you tell me why the Songbird Cafe is so important to Little Bird?"

For a second I can't speak. My heart is pounding in my ears and my palms feel sticky. And then I spot Flora. She's moved so that she's standing directly behind Davida.

"Look at me," she mouths, pointing to herself. "Tell me."

I focus on Flora. "We don't need a big hotel on the island that brings in tourists for a few months of the year," I hear myself say. "We need somewhere special to meet every day, somewhere there's a friendly face and a warm welcome. I'm new to this island, but the cafe is already an important part of my life. It's like in that film, *Breakfast at Tiffany's*, when Audrey Hepburn says that nothing bad ever happens at Tiffany's. That's what the cafe is like. It's a place where you can forget about your worries and have some delicious cake and hot chocolate. Everyone needs somewhere like the Songbird Cafe. Somewhere you feel at home.

"And this island is part of history. My ancestor Red Moll lived up there." I point to the castle peeking out over the Songbird's roof. "She defended the people of this island from slave traders," I continue. "They can't build a big hotel in front of her castle – it just isn't right. So I'm asking people to help us fight to keep the cafe open."

Davida smiles at me. "Thank you, Mollie. An eloquent plea indeed."

The crowd claps and cheers their support – apart from Lauren, of course, who is rolling her eyes. Flora nods at me and beams. Then I spot Alanna. Her eyes are welling up with tears again. She blows me a kiss. Flora puts her arm around Alanna's waist and gives her a squeeze.

"And how can people show their support for the campaign, Mollie?" Davida asks me.

"We have a Save the Songbird Cafe Facebook page you can like," I say. "And you can sign our online petition and make a donation."

"Thank you, Mollie. Now back to the studio for more local news." Davida waits for a few seconds and then says, "And cut." She turns to me. "You were wonderful. Well done. Your mum must be very proud of you."

"You were brilliant, Mollie," Bonny says, coming up to me. "And I'm sorry about Nan. I hope she gets better soon."

"Thanks, Bonny," I say. "Nan's much better. She's coming home later, in fact."

"Why are you talking to *her*?" Lauren scowls at Bonny.

"I can talk to whoever I want, Lauren," Bonny says, going a little red. I can tell she's still nervous of Lauren and I don't blame her.

But suddenly I realize that I'm not frightened of Lauren any more and her mean comments don't bother me. "You have no power here," I tell her. "Begone, before somebody drops a house on you too."

Bonny laughs. "*The Wizard of Oz*, right? Great film."

Lauren is glaring at me. "You are so weird, Molly Cinnamon. And, Bonny, if you're coming back to my place, you have to come now." She flounces off with Chloe at her heels.

"Mollie," Bonny says quietly, "about all that school stuff. No one believes Lauren. About you pushing her. You could come back if you wanted to."

"Thanks, Bonny."

She smiles at me. "You really were great. Good luck with the campaign. I'd better go, but maybe we can watch that movie together some time." She runs after Lauren.

"Bye, Bonny," I call after her. "I'd like that."

Flora comes over then and gives me a hug. "You were amazing, darling, a natural."

"She's a credit to you, Flora," Lucas says. "I can't believe you have a daughter who's so grown up. You only look like a teenager yourself."

Flora slaps him on the arm. "Stop! You kidder." But she's clearly delighted.

"It must be cool having such a young mum," Davida says. "And don't worry, Mollie – I'll make sure this goes out this evening. You have my word. Hey, Flora, do you have time for a coffee and a quick catch-up?"

"Why don't you come to the house?" Flora says. "I know Lucas wants to see some of Mollie's footage of the island. He can edit the piece from up there and send it straight to the studio."

Davida smiles. "Sounds like a plan."

Mattie gives Lucas and Davida a lift to Nan's house as they have a lot of equipment to carry. Flora and I walk up together. At the end of the lane, she stops and says, "I've been thinking."

"Don't do too much of that, Flora," I say with a grin. "You might injure yourself."

"Ha ha! But seriously. I want you to know I'm very proud of you. And I really will try harder to put you first."

I bump her with my shoulder. "OK, Mum."

She grins and bumps me back. "You know what, I actually quite like the sound of that. And being your mum is pretty cool."

Chapter 20

At six o'clock we all gather in Nan's living room to watch the news on her big telly: me, Flora, Alanna, Landy and Sunny. Sadly Lucas and Davida had to get back to Dublin. Alanna has prepared some finger food especially and I help her spread it out on the coffee table: tiny samosas the size of butterfly wings, smoked-salmon blinis, spicy guacamole with tortillas to dip into it, mini ham-and-cheese quiches. It all smells delicious.

"Tuck in, everyone," Alanna says.

I try to eat a samosa, but I'm so nervous about the news piece – that they won't show it, that they will show it and it won't make any difference, the cafe will still close – that it tastes like cardboard in my mouth.

The news crawls by and I can hardly bear the wait. Landy is sitting on the sofa with Nan's laptop on his knee. He has our Save the Songbird Cafe Facebook page open, and he's ready to answer any viewers' questions. That was Flora's idea – she's surprisingly clued up when it comes to social media. She says having a public face is part of her presenting job and Lucas is helping her set up her own *Travelling Light* social media accounts. She also put a PayPal button on the cafe's website, so that people can make online donations, and then she linked the button to the Facebook page. She's thought of everything.

But it doesn't look like there will be any questions. "They're not going to show it," I say despondently.

"It'll be on," Flora says. "Davida promised."

At quarter to seven there's the sound of a car pulling up outside and then voices in the hall. Nan hurries into the living room, followed by Bat.

"Have we missed the bit about the cafe?" Nan asks urgently.

"Nan!" I run over and give her a hug. "How are you feeling? Are you well enough to be out of hospital?"

"Good to see you, child. And I'm fine. Nothing that a bit of rest won't cure."

"Sit down, Nan. It'll be on any moment now." Flora gives Nan her seat and perches on the arm of the chair beside her. Bat squeezes onto the sofa.

"It's wonderful to see you, Nan," Alanna says. "We've all missed you. Oh, wait. Look! It's on."

I look back at the TV and there it is – the Songbird Cafe. I squeal. "Turn it up, Flora," I say, fizzing with excitement.

As Flora adjusts the volume, Davida's voice rings out. "This is Davida Walsh, reporting from Little Bird Island, where the local community are campaigning to save their only cafe. Alanna D'Arcy, you own and run the Songbird Cafe, is that correct?"

As the camera swings over to Alanna we all cheer.

"Yes," we hear Alanna say. "I took a loan out with the bank to pay for some building work and, to cut a long story short, they want their money back, pronto. They're putting pressure on me to sell to a developer. If I just had a bit more time, I'd happily pay it back. I'm not looking for charity."

"And the developers intend to demolish the cafe and build a large hotel in its place?"

Alanna nods. "Sadly, yes."

Then I see my own face on screen. My big white face, framed by wild red curls, whipping around like kite tails in the wind.

Everyone in the room cheers again.

"Go, Mollie!" Landy calls.

"Shush," Nan says. "I want to hear this."

It's unreal listening to myself answer all Davida's questions and explain about Red Moll's castle. When I've finished speaking, they show a short montage of film clips set to music – birds swooping in the sky, Click jumping out of the waves, and a girl in a red cloak set against Red Moll's castle – and suddenly I realize why it all looks so familiar.

"It's your footage, Mollie!" Flora squeals. "Your work is on national television."

"And that's me," Alanna says. "In the red cloak."

"It's amazing, Mollie," Nan says proudly. "My girls have such talent."

I feel dizzy with relief. They played it. Our campaign was on the news!

"Oh, Mollie, Alanna, what can I say?" Nan says. "You were both wonderful. I think I speak for everyone when I say well done. And to Sunny, Landy and all of you behind the scenes. And to clever old Flora for getting it on the news. Whatever happens now, you've all done Little Bird proud."

"Nan's right," Alanna says. "Thank you everyone for fighting for the cafe."

"So what now?" I ask.

"We wait," Flora says. "Any reaction on the Facebook page yet, Landy?"

He shakes his head. "Not yet. Oh, hang on. We have three new likes. And a new comment. It says, 'I've signed your petition and I've made an online donation. Good luck with your campaign. Little Bird is a very special place.'"

"There'll be more," Flora says. "Wait and see."

Flora's right. An hour later, the Facebook likes are still coming in. We're at over three hundred now. And the donations are up to four hundred euros. Everyone has gone home, but Flora, Nan and I are still in the living room, celebrating the success of the news piece and Nan's return. Flora has taken over from Landy on laptop duty.

"There's a private message here for Alanna from a Cathy Mullins, CEO of Haven Foods," she says. "Her son Teddy visited the cafe recently with his grandparents and hasn't stopped going on about it since. She's interested in talking to her about a possible sponsorship deal."

"Sounds promising," Nan says. Then she gives a huge yawn. "Too much excitement for one day, I'm afraid. I'm off to bed now."

"Of course, Nan," Flora says. "You must be exhausted. The doctor did tell you to take it easy. You tired, Mopsy? It's been quite a day."

"A little," I admit. And then I realize we've been so caught up in the cafe and the news that we haven't talked about the other thing that's on my mind – staying here or going home with Flora. I know I have to tell them my decision. "Flora, have you talked to Nan about the extra filming?" I ask.

"She has," Nan says. "And you're welcome to stay for as long as you want, Mollie. I adore having you here – you know that. If you'd like to stay, then we can work out all the details later. But the important thing is I love you and I want to be part of your life and spend as much time with you as I can. It's as simple as that. We have a lot of classic movies to watch."

Flora laughs. "Not you too. I guess that's where Mum got her movie-star obsession."

"I take it you're not a fan of old films?" Nan says.

"No, but a girl can change."

"Indeed she can."

Flora looks at me now, her face getting serious. "What would you like to do, Mopsy? Stay here with Nan or go back to Dublin with me? It's completely up to you, darling. Have you thought about it?"

I nod. I've been thinking about it a lot. But in the end it all came down to one thing – Flora. You see, I know how much she loves her job. Being a television presenter is all she's ever wanted to do. Offering to leave her dream job was the most amazingly kind thing ever. It would be like me offering never to watch another movie again in my whole entire life (which I honestly think would kill me).

I know if I asked her to leave *Travelling Light*, she would. But I can't do it. Because she's my mum and I love her and I want her to be happy. I know she said she was sick of travelling, but once she's filming again she'll forget about all that. And this time she'll have Lucas to look after her.

Besides, I'm starting to feel like I belong here. I never, ever in a million years thought I'd say it, but it's true. I like Little Bird! Yes, it's quiet and small and there are no shops. But it's beautiful, and there's a very special cafe, and amazing people that I'd like to get to know better, like Landy and Sunny. And Alanna. Most of all, Alanna. I want to spend more time with Nan too and be a proper great-granddaughter.

And there's one final reason.

I dreamed about Granny Ellen last night. We were standing in front of Red Moll's castle and she was telling me a Red Moll story, about how when she was only nine Red Moll saved one of her sisters from drowning. She jumped into the sea after her and dragged her to shore. We were holding hands and the wind was blowing our red hair behind us as we stared out to sea.

"We're islanders," Granny Ellen said. "No matter how far

away we are, Little Bird will always be our home."

I wish Granny Ellen was still alive. I miss her every single day. I think she would want me to stay and keep an eye on Nan. I think she's somewhere up there, looking out for us both, our very own red-haired angel.

So I nod and say, "Yes. I've made a decision."

Epilogue

On Mother's Day I'm in the kitchen of the Songbird Cafe with Alanna, stirring the chocolate fudge cake mix. I sent Flora a Mother's Day e-card this morning. When you open it, "Somewhere Over the Rainbow" plays and bluebirds and butterflies flutter across the screen. I hope she likes it.

I made a real card for Nan. I took a photo of some daffodils in her garden. Then I printed it and stuck it on card and decorated the edges. Sunny helped me with the calligraphy inside. You should have seen the one Sunny made. She'd copied a picture of her mum from a photograph and it was amazing. She's so talented. I'm lucky to have her as a friend.

Cathy from Haven Foods was as good as her word. She came to see the cafe and to talk to Alanna. Her company agreed to sponsor the Songbird and she offered to help Alanna get back on her feet by mentoring her, so the cafe's future is safe. There's now a large plaque that reads "Sponsored by Haven Foods" by the cafe door and Alanna has dedicated a new cupcake to Cathy's son Teddy – the Teddy Treat. It's a vanilla cupcake decorated with sprinkles, Smarties and jelly dolphins.

I work for Alanna every weekend and on Wednesday afternoons when there's no school. I thought going back to Bethlehem Heights would be difficult, but, in fact, as long as I avoid Lauren, it's actually not that bad. Bonny's really kind and Landy's great fun to hang out with.

"I've been meaning to ask you, sparrow," Alanna says, after tasting the cake mix. "The day you came to the island I saw you make a wish on a straw doll. Did it ever come true?"

So much has happened since then, but I can still remember my wish. *Take me home.*

"Yes, I guess it did." For the moment, Little Bird is my home and, as Dorothy says in *The Wizard of Oz*, there's no place like it.

"Magic," she says, smiling, and leaves it at that. But from the twinkle in her eyes, I'm sure she's reading my mind again.

Five things you might not know about me

by Mollie Cinnamon

1. My favourite movie is *The Wizard of Oz*.

2. I have not one but two favourite colours – black *and* white. Stripes. I love zebra stripes.

3. I can touch my nose with my tongue and curl it. Those are pretty special talents!

4. I love the smell of baking, especially cupcakes.

5. If I could have any super power, it would be flight. Or invisibility. Or both!

My top five movies ⭐

by Mollie Cinnamon

1. *The Wizard of Oz* is the best movie ever. "Lions and tigers, and bears (oh my!)" and so much more. Don't miss it!

2. *Spirited Away* is an amazing animated movie from Japan. I could watch it over and over again.

3. *Grease* has brilliant songs and a fantastic story. Yes, I have a bit of a thing for musicals!

4. *E.T. the Extra-Terrestrial* is about the cutest alien ever. It's also the cutest friendship movie you'll ever watch.

5. *Beetlejuice* is the best comedy-ghost movie in the world.

I also love *Ghostbusters*, *Annie* and *The Princess Bride*. Old movies rule!

Recipe for the Songbird Cupcake

by Alanna D'Arcy

Ingredients

For the cupcakes (makes 12):

2 eggs

110g self-raising flour

110g butter

110g caster sugar

2 tsp baking powder

For the icing:

220g icing sugar

110g butter

Blue food colouring

Instructions

1. Ask a parent or guardian to preheat the oven to 180°C.

2. Place 12 paper cupcake cases on a tray.

3. Mix the sugar, flour and baking powder together. Then add the butter and eggs.

4. Stir all of the ingredients together until the mixture is pale and fluffy.

5. Spoon the mixture into the paper cases.

6. Ask a parent or guardian to put the tray of cases into the oven.

7. Bake the cakes for around 15 minutes or until they are golden brown. Ask a parent or guardian to help with this.

8. Once cooked, allow the cakes to cool.

9. To make the icing, whisk the butter and sugar together.

10. Add a couple of drops of blue food colouring to the butter-sugar mix.

11. Ask a parent or guardian to help you cut a circle out of the top of each cake. Fill this hole with icing.

12. Place the cut-out cake pieces on top of the icing to look like wings.

Interview with Sarah Webb

(author of The Songbird Cafe Girls)

1. Little Bird is such a lovely place. Was it inspired by a real island?

Yes, it was inspired by two islands off West Cork, Ireland: Cape Clear and Sherkin Island. I wanted to create somewhere very beautiful and quite magical, like those real islands. But I also wanted to give Little Bird, rapids, its own dolphin (called Click) and its own special atmosphere.

2. This book is about finding a place in the world that feels like home. Where is your favourite place?

A tiny village in West Cork called Castletownshend. The scenery is stunning and it's right on the sea. I love swimming and kayaking and sailing, so it suits me perfectly. I do a lot of my writing there.

3. Who was your best friend at school?

I had two best friends the whole way through school, and they are still my best friends now. I met them through sailing. They are called Nicky and Tanya, and they are funny and beautiful and super smart! (They made me say that, but it's true!)

4. Mollie's favourite film is *The Wizard of Oz*. What's yours?

Like Mollie, I'm a big movie fan. In fact, we share a lot of favourites, including *The Wizard of Oz* and *Spirited Away*. I also love *Field of Dreams*. I watch it every year because it reminds me to have big dreams and to follow my heart.

5. Flora loves her job as a TV presenter. If you weren't an author, what would you be?

A children's bookseller. My dream is to run my own children's bookshop one day. Watch this space!

6. Which character from *Mollie Cinnamon Is Not a Cupcake* are you most like?

That's a hard question. I guess, if I had to pick one, I'd say Nan. She's a lot older than I am, but like me, she makes mistakes and attempts to fix them as best she can. She also fights for what she believes in and tries to look after the people she loves.

7. We have loved reading about Mollie, Landy, Sunny and Alanna. Can we expect more stories about them?

Yes, there are two more books to come, *Sunny Days and Mooncakes* – which is about Mollie's friend, Sunny – and the third book, which is about Rory, a girl who befriends Click the dolphin.

Acknowledgements

A book is very much like a small island. It cannot survive without people to care for it and love it. I'm very lucky to have an editor who truly cares about my writing, the wonderful Annalie. (She even provided the delicious Songbird Cupcake recipe!) She was ably helped by Emily, and Maria, who worked terribly hard on the cover, and Jack, who created the map.

Thanks must also go to the rest of the stellar team at Walker Books, especially the majestic Conor, my man on the ground in Ireland, plus Paul, Gill, Jo, Victoria and Heidi. Thanks also to Philippa and Peta, my wonderful agents.

To my family, as always – for putting up with me. Living with a writer is no joke and no woman is an island! And to Helen, for taking such good care of Amy and Jago while I write. And to my writer friends, for listening to all my plot woes, especially Martina, Clare, Judi and Marita.

To the booksellers, far and wide, who have supported my books for many years, especially the gang at Dubray Books, David O'C at Eason, Louisa and Kim at Raven, Bob and gang at Gutter, Mary Brigid at Hodges Figgis, and all at Bridge Street Books.

To the hard-working ladies at Children's Books Ireland, the lads and lasses at the Irish Writers' Centre, and Marian, Bert and Alice at the Mountains to Sea Book Festival, who I have the great pleasure of working with.

Clodagh Walsh, winner of my Young Editor Competition, gave me some super-smart feedback on this book. The future of literature is in good hands.

And finally I'd like to thank you for picking up Mollie's story. Books only truly come alive when they are read.

I love hearing from readers. Do drop me a line – sarah@sarahwebb.ie.

Yours in books,
Sarah XXX

Sarah Webb worked as a children's bookseller for many years before becoming a full-time writer. Writing is her dream job because it means she can travel, read books and magazines, watch movies, and interrogate friends and family, all in the name of "research". She adores stationery, especially stickers, and is a huge reader – she reads at least one book a week. As well as The Songbird Cafe Girls series, Sarah has written six Ask Amy Green books, eleven adult novels and many books for younger children. She visits a school every Friday during term time and loves meeting young readers and writers. She has been shortlisted for the Queen of Teen Award (twice!) and the Irish Book Awards.

Find out more about Sarah at www.SarahWebb.ie or on Twitter (@sarahwebbishere) and facebook.com/sarahwebbwriter.

Don't miss the next book about
the Songbird Cafe Girls

SUNNY
DAYS
AND MOON
CAKES